PLOUGHSHARES

Spring 1994 · Vol. 20, No. 1

GUEST EDITOR
James Welch

EXECUTIVE DIRECTOR
DeWitt Henry

MANAGING EDITOR *&* FICTION EDITOR
Don Lee

POETRY EDITOR
David Daniel

ASSISTANT EDITOR
Jessica Dineen

EDITORIAL ASSISTANT
Stephanie Booth

FOUNDING PUBLISHER
Peter O'Malley

PLOUGHSHARES, a journal of new writing, is guest-edited serially by prominent writers who explore different and personal visions, aesthetics, and literary circles. PLOUGHSHARES is published in April, August, and December at Emerson College, 100 Beacon Street, Boston, MA 02116-1596. Telephone: (617) 578-8753. Phone-a-Poem: (617) 578-8754.

STAFF ASSISTANT: Jodee Stanley. INTERNS: Kristen Cudmore and George Carner. POETRY READERS: Mary-Margaret Mulligan, Linda Russo, Karen Voelker, Jason Rogers, Tom Laughlin, Renee Rooks, Bill Keeney, Susan Rich, Rachel Piccione, and Bethany Daniel. FICTION READERS: Billie Lydia Porter, Michael Rainho, Lee Harrington, Stephanie Booth, Jodee Stanley, Karen Wise, Esther Crain, Christine Flanagan, Maryanne O'Hara, Kim Reynolds, David Rowell, Holly LeCraw Howe, Sara Nielsen Gambrill, Tanja Brull, and Barbara Lewis. PHONE-A-POEM COORDINATOR: Joyce Peseroff.

SUBSCRIPTIONS (ISSN 0048-4474): $19/domestic and $24/international for individuals; $22/domestic and $27/international for institutions. See last page for order form.

UPCOMING: Fall 1994, Vol. 20, Nos. 2 & 3, a special issue of personal narratives edited by Rosellen Brown, will appear in August 1994. Winter 1994-95, Vol. 20, No. 4, a staff-edited poetry and fiction issue, will appear in December 1994. Both issues are editorially complete.

SUBMISSIONS: Please see back of issue for detailed submission policies.

BACK ISSUES are available from the publisher. Write or call for abstracts and a price list. Microfilms of back issues may be obtained from University Microfilms. PLOUGHSHARES is also available as a CD-ROM full-text product from UMI and Information Access Company. INDEXED in M.L.A. Bibliography, American Humanities Index, Index of American Periodical Verse, Book Review Index. Self-index through Volume 6 available from the publisher; annual supplements appear in the fourth number of each subsequent volume. All rights for individual works revert to the authors upon publication.

DISTRIBUTED by Bernhard DeBoer (113 E. Centre St., Nutley, NJ 07110), Fine Print Distributors (6448 Highway 290 East, Austin, TX 78723), Ingram Periodicals (1226 Heil Quaker Blvd., La Vergne, TN 37086), Inland Book Co. (140 Commerce St., East Haven, CT 06523), and L-S Distributors (130 East Grand Ave., South San Francisco, CA 94080). PRINTED by Edwards Brothers.

PLOUGHSHARES receives additional support from the Lannan Foundation, the National Endowment for the Arts, and the Massachusetts Cultural Council. Major new marketing initiatives have been made possible by the Lila Wallace–Reader's Digest Literary Publishers Marketing Development Program, funded through a grant to the Council of Literary Magazines and Presses. The opinions expressed in this magazine do not necessarily reflect those of Emerson College, the editors, the staff, the trustees, or the supporting organizations.

CONTENTS

Ploughshares · Spring 1994

Introduction

Twenty-five years ago a poet from Ireland came to the University of Montana to replace Richard Hugo for a year. Hugo had a Rockefeller and he was going to spend a year in Italy to work on a book of poems based on his World War II experience as a bombardier, flying missions out of Italy. That book would become *Good Luck in Cracked Italian*.

I was one of the students that the Irish poet, Anthony Cronin, inherited, and he was quite pleased that I had an American Indian heritage and identified myself as an Indian. But he wondered how an Indian could have a name like Welch. That was an Irish name. I told him that I had two Irish grandfathers and one Blackfeet and one Gros Ventre grandmother. But it wasn't quite that simple. One of my grandfathers came out west as an Indian agent from North Carolina and had a Cherokee princess in his ancestry. Surprisingly, this Irish poet seemed to know about Cherokee princesses.

One night about a week later, Tony hurried into Eddy's Club, a local writer/graduate student/hippie haunt, and pulled out a slick chunk of paper and unfolded it before me. It was a map of Ireland and it took up the whole table. He pointed to a spot along the southern coast and said, "That's where you're from! That's where the Welch tribe originated!" He'd already been drinking and his smudgy glasses were down on the end of his nose, but his eyes were triumphant, almost defiant. I was young and I didn't know whether to be flattered that he had taken the time to show me my Irish origins or to be alarmed at his insistence that I know them. And in truth I had never identified with the Irish. I had grown up as an Indian, as a member of two Indian tribes. All my relatives were Indians.

Later that night, as I crossed the snowy bridge over the Clark Fork River, I began to think of my new Irish tribe—must have been the Celts—and of all the tribes in the world: European tribes, the Goths, the Franks, the Picts, Middle Eastern tribes, the Lost Tribes of Israel, Far Eastern Tribes, desert tribes, the Ainus of Japan, Mongolians, Genghis Khan, the tribes of Africa, Watusis, Zulus, the tribes of Southeast Asia and South America, some of whom were still being "discovered." Even in my beery state, or perhaps because of it, I was thrilled by the notion of a world full of tribes. It had been that way once upon a time. In some parts of the world, in spite of political boundaries, people still identify themselves according to family, clan, band, society, tribe. They still depend upon collective memory, spirituality, environmental lightness, and group loyalty to perpetrate their way of life.

It is sad to think that one day there will be no more tribes as we know them. There are too many anthropologists and missionaries out there looking to study and convert them. There are too many oil companies, lumber companies, soda pop companies, looking to exploit them. We will introduce them to the luxuries of civilization. Then we will try to figure out why they were so happy then and so unhappy now.

When *Ploughshares* very kindly invited me to be guest editor of this issue, I was asked to come up with a theme that not only would have something to do with my own background but might have a kind of universal appeal—hence, tribe. In my call to writers, I offered a definition of "tribe" that I found in my old *Webster's Seventh New Collegiate Dictionary: 1. A social group comprising numerous families, clans, or generations together with slaves, dependents, or adopted strangers. 2. A group of persons having a common character, occupation, or interest.*

But what is our notion of tribe and tribalism as we approach the twenty-first century? Perhaps not strangely, many of the poems and stories I received peck around the edges of both definitions. Writers are notoriously, triumphantly, on the edge of established society—it sometimes seems they can only comment on society from the fringes. This is not to say that writers do not go to church or become members of the PTA, but very few of them will bake a cake to send the high school band to Pasadena. This kind of rah-rah tribalism doesn't interest them as parents and citizens. But that doesn't mean they can't write a sexy account of such an activity.

Many of the stories and poems are about war—literal, sociopolitical, and domestic—with varying points of view, from those of abusers to victims to bystanders. Some of the work directly portrays ethnic tribes. Whether Haitian, Latino, Asian American, or Native American, these writers proudly describe their own cultures, with an underlying realization and sadness that they are being swallowed up by the dominant culture, rather than being accepted by it.

Other variations on the theme of tribes include homosexuality, love, religion. One poet writes of leaving the tribe of nuns before the final initiation. Another poet deals with homosexuality in the military—a tribe within a tribe. A story speaks chillingly of a female bodybuilder who identifies more with a group of transvestites on a park bench than with her fellow bank employees. What nearly all of these works share is the desire to acknowledge the tribes of people outside the cozy confines of larger society and their inalienable right to bang at the gates.

Admittedly, there are several poets and storytellers in this issue who strain *Webster's* definition of tribe. They are simply good. The tribe of good writing.

ELIZABETH WOODY

The Girlfriends

Filled with old lovers, in the clutch of the chair,
you are a bloom of uncombed hair.

With a collection of roses, bowls of mashed petals,
I make a clear cup of sky.
Fold away clouds. Roll up blankets of blue.
I am a body of empty husks.
Indian corn is in your hair, the tassels,
the pollen, fertility.

Indelible ink is tattooing our lungs.
We speak smoke.
We exchange our lunacy for reverence.
Respect tornadoes.
Windy Woman. Four Winds.

We have extended the edge of expectations
by merely living.

You have tallied compulsion
into currency.
I am measured by the excitement
my lips stir.
I am the bin for castoffs and the weary.
I wear my veil.
I have no children,
but you have many.
You dream of heaven and they all run up to meet you.

Perfidy

A few sounds, over and again, grip me through this
    drunken mess.
I walk to the oblivious road, gone and done for.
A few beats of my pulse splinter through the plates
    of my skull.
The gun blast, I do not know where the bullet hit
or the depth of my wound.
My children, I regress.
I pray to Our Father, see Daddy.
Mother does not condemn.

I have fruit so sweet with youth,
who are daughters, opposite
of self, like naiveté and craziness.

In the gentle possession of touch,
a hardened lullaby,
I see my daughters as magnets, together.
One large, one small.
I blow against the Cyclone fence
and their unfailing grief and affection.

The television tells of my charm against calamity.
How the large Indian female
shot in the head, late twenties, escapes
police guard and the university hospital.
The eldest daughter's skin shivers as she prays,
"If I die before I wake..."

The brain ferments itself out of pain.
I will not say who is the perpetrator.
I want to know the one face is free
to see the dead return.
The head wound is inconsequential.

My hair curls out white,
feathers over my angelic face.

I am an abrasive pendulum
swinging back and forth, hypnotic
as a knife.

My reprisal is only to live
and grow into my daughters.

Straight and Clear

I.

Between the confluence of the rivers, the smolt twist and die
in massive turbines. Liaison between the proliferation,
Nusoox and all the commissions, Yowanswickt watches the roll
of dice, pitched in bone games, about irrigation, treaty
and young, vulnerable fish. Dialogues with usurpers
who are loquacious and convinced of the real in terms of
debt and waste, he bargains with one foot in lineage,
the other in goodwill. Through the languages' power
of connection, words make the river water flowing, into time,
entitles the glacier water, becomes the clouds, the land absorbing
light an obvious promotion of value beyond just conference.
Reduction is the paper talk of minimum usage. The passage
is congruity.

II.

The Eagle rests on the freeway lamp posts, listens
to the senseless dirge of irony and air brakes.
She wobbles in takeoff between magnificence and the Moon.
Her contention is that one must feed the children first.
Road kill or dove.

III.

The uncut hair moves over his suit jacket. His intonation is passionate
in the discussion, he says, "If they live, we live, and if not,
we perish." Indicator species are passed off as unwilling
change in management of our resources. Evidence is intangible
but bold print of CANCER collects itself in the down winders
of the Hanford Nuclear Reservation. The difficult colloquies
of a people who are marked as the expendables. Radiation
of the dispossessed sting from removal, one by one
into absolute silence. The words are not easy for my dear cousin,

forty-three, who did not drink or smoke, as she
calmly says in her soft voice, "This is the last night
I will be able to speak." These are the last words as
another woman continues in her stead, will not shut up,
fearful of the silence. No one interrupts this friend
out of politeness. The next morning, my cousin's throat and songs
are no longer among the family as prayer.

IV.

We are living in the soil, part tree, a bed of free creek,
the head of volcanoes that weep stream. Divided in parts
the plates shake, rain does not come. We are not noble
or indivisible, but practitioners of words so strong,
they cannot be written. The words can only live
as each being who lives is an anomaly to the futility
of these systems that have decreed death. Death masks
encroachment without respect. The words are the core
of the tree that represents the elder government of this
continent. The ignoble savage may only be a founding father,
a Washington or Franklin on the dollar bill describing
itself, the hands it has changed.

V.

He paints hands, the signature of the unwritten heritage,
over and over, growing larger each year, until a document
as large as a canyon wall is signed by this method, the hands
    of The People,
who are not X's on treaty or land sale. The hands are presence,
action, as well as tool for rebuilding from the wreckage.

VI.

It is not ease or congratulatory gestures that enable
men to grow, who are men of the land. The smell of fire smoke
and salmon are worn as the cape of princehood. Pita's questions
are not out of proportion when the child asks about the

return of ancestral bones moved from Memaloose Island.
In fairness, he asks about the poor "whiteman" left behind,
who chose to be buried with the "Indians." In case the dead rise
at Armageddon, he trusted his soul and chances with the humble
house of bones. Separation occurs between the prominent
figure and our anonymous bones, inundated in prophecy by
the hydroelectric dams. The child asks for the return
of his ancestors' bones, because it all seems so unfair.
The skulls in the black-and-white photo postcard stare
into his chest, femur bones are crossed recklessly,
not religious.

On the drive to the point in Chewana where Tsagagllallal
looks over the backwaters, an old rattlesnake presents himself.
The son and father hang over him from the car.
The son says, "What an *Old* Grandfather!"

The Snake: "I am old because I am connected in all my parts
to the earth. I feel the vibration of the center,
so I coil and roll on to the river, not ambivalent."
The river that motions itself in the directions of forever.
The past is itself, is an ocean, is the self, cloud,
is the absorption into these men.

VII.

Crying to the uncle of a love gone awry, he says,
"It is the hardest thing for a young woman to learn
the difference between a man who is thoughtless
from one who takes action from his heart..."
Is it the man inside that cannot make a decision,
or is it the woman inside who cannot decide
if we need more takers or creators?
The land bends its back to accommodate the monolithic
presence of volcanoes and the atomic reactors.
"The woman chooses, always chooses."

VIII.

The wheels have four parts, North, East, South, West.
The wheels that move so freely across this land turn
so ludicrous in enmity, disturbing the peace of the Holy Wheel.
Still, the men are dancing somewhere,
presenting argument over there,
clasping the belly of a wife, possibly
enclosing their brood in their arms and teaching,
"It is all right to cry, because you have a heart,
and the tears stop it from having the pressure
build from forgetting to care."

The earth is a shield, the drum of love,
the first murmur, the terror,
a powerful woman who whispers
into his ears at night.
Vision is not dream, but the absolute mind viewing
continuity, itself, straight in the clear circle.

from *Perma Red*

Bad Ways

On the Flathead Reservation you can come to a spot in the
road where the wind smells like sulfur, a dark smell, something you think you should be able to leave behind you, but it will
be in your clothing and in your shoes. And there will be a darkness in the way you see things, a darkness you wish you could
leave. The Indians say it is because of the old white-man ghost
that haunts the Dixon side of the river, the old white-man ghost
that rode through the land before Dixon was a town, because
there were some Indians a long time ago and these Indians had
listened to too many white men and they had found themselves
hungry with only empty pockets of land, land that had a stinging
edge, a bitter taste like the silt dark water on a beaver pond, a land
they couldn't leave, or see beyond, or even move for a short time,
a land where the dark fish began leaving the rivers as if they were
being washed away by an angry, pulling current.

This was an end to the land, they told themselves, and not
because their enemy the Blackfeet pressed in on them but because
the land itself was being corralled. They had seen more than deer
caught on the miles of thorn wire. They had seen small bundles
tied tight with strands of horse hair and for the first time they
didn't know who had placed the small bundles around them. It
was a medicine that called them to bad dreams and woke them
dry-mouthed and praying. And they knew that whoever had put
the small bundles on the ripping wire was afraid of more than
small hunger, whoever had left the bundles was afraid of a with-
ering heat that could speak to them at night like a bad animal
caught in their throats, afraid of old power dying on their
tongues so that day by day their people would begin to stink with
loss. And the power did leave. And these Indians so long ago had
to bury their shit because they were locked in small pieces of

land, because their skin began to itch and the soles of their feet burned, because the strands of their hair lined with small white eggs. And a deep hunger made them small and so hungry, at night they dreamed of small bits of food in the mouths of birds, so hungry the sides of their bellies bloated like deer and their ribs became hard. And when they slept, they slept on soil or cattails ground to pitiful dust by the stiff bones of their asses because in their hunger they tried eating their elk blanket robes by boiling them clean in water. But the elk hide was thick and the water in which they boiled the hides stayed flat and bitter. The water did not foam up with the sweet smell of bone marrow. Then the hides turned green and the elk died twice.

When the white man came, he came with a shining watch, gold lined the back of his teeth, and he liked to smile because of it. He told these hungry Indians, the whole time playing with the coins in his pockets, that he wanted to play a gambling game with them, an Indian gambling game, and in exchange he'd like to get himself an Indian woman. And the Indian men laughed because all of their women were so hard you could count their bones. They had lost their breasts, and their hair was coarse from lack of any oil.

"Just the same," the white man had told them, "I want one of your women."

And the Indian men, the few that would talk to him, were curious about this. They wanted to know what he wanted with their women. The white man looked them straight on.

"I don't care who she is," he said. "She can be ugly or beautiful. I want her to dance for me. I want her to dance like a small deer for me alone."

Then the white man winked at the Indian men and they were not sure what he meant by this gesture though they knew it meant more than what he was saying. Still they never thought to ask what it was exactly that the white man wanted. He wanted it all, they believed, to lie with an Indian woman in tall grass, to press into her, to sleep. They were only thinking of the bright gold at the cuff of his sleeve, the blinding white stones in his rings, his pockets deep with coins.

Some of these Indian men began to think about this.

"What game could we play with you?" they asked him.

The white man was quiet. He shrugged his shoulders as if he didn't have a game in mind, as if he didn't know how to win. The Indians named off stick games and foot races, story games and mazes. The white man put his hands on his hips and looked at the ground. And these Indians began to feel bad, thinking maybe this white man couldn't gamble with them. Then they mentioned hunting games and fishing.

"I will fish," the white man said. "I will fish these waters and I will fish by myself and I will bring in more fish than all five of you. And if we fish a draw," he said, "you will have my money. All my money."

And these few Indian men looked at each other not wanting to smile and show the white man they had already won this game.

"Okay," they said, "you go on and fish, but fish by yourself," they said, feeling their winnings. "And if you only catch one fish, one big fish, you win."

"Well," said the white man, "you are being more than fair, but I must ask for the company of an Indian woman while I sit by the riverbank fishing."

The Indian men looked at one another. This request did not seem so unreasonable. Their hesitation must have seemed like reluctance to the white man.

"Here," he said to them, "you can hold on to my horse until I return."

"We don't need your horse," they said, because they believed that they were winning.

So these Indian men, the ones that were talking to the white man, began listing all the women in the camp. They thought of Broken Feet and Long Man's daughter. They thought of Small Salmon, how she was graceful and quick and pregnant. They thought of a woman who liked to sleep with all the men in camp, and laughed to recall she smelled like river mud and onions. They thought of Humming Blood but knew she wasn't right in the head. Then they thought of White Crow. She wasn't pretty and no man had spoken for her. She was quiet and never talked. She wouldn't complain if they forced her favor. They began wondering why she had been overlooked for so long, why Long Man had not made her more available. The Indian men snuck up close to White Crow and were surprised when she smiled at them, pleased at all the attention they were giving her. She stood up proudly and walked down the river to meet the white man. The Indian men waved White Crow on and sat down to wait for their treasures.

They sat a long time. They looked towards the river and talked among themselves. They wanted to feel the heavy coins in their hands. One talked about the gold watch and how he would smash the face to stop the white man's time. They laughed at this, stopping time. They looked at the sun. Much time had passed. They did not tell this white man he had to be back by a certain time. They worried a little. Maybe they should try to catch a few fish. Maybe he was already having such a good time with White Crow he wasn't going to come back and settle his bet. Maybe he had already gotten what he wanted while they sat in camp waiting like fools. They remembered White Crow waving to them, White Crow walking to the river. They began talking about how pretty she was and how they had overlooked her for too long. They got it in their minds that they should go see what was going on with the white man and White Crow.

When they saw the river and the white man's horse, they hunkered down behind the river brush, watching for the two of them, White Crow and the white man. But they only saw the white man sitting close to the water, and beside him were larger fish than they had seen in a long time. They went down to the white man, admiring his fish. And he tossed the fish over to them. Fish flapped on the dry rocks in front of the Indians. Fish, their puffing gills powdered in dust, their green tails sweet and slick. Fat fish the length of a short man's legs. The white man smiled at these Indians. The Indians looked at each other and smiled at the fish. For so long the river had run dry of food. The Indians forgot all about White Crow, so busy they were with all they thought they were gaining. All of them hungry with the hope of fish.

"What are you doing to get these big fish?" they asked the white man. "We have tried everything but our peckers."

They laughed and the white man laughed, too. And they laughed harder as he lifted his hand and pointed down past the big rock where his silver line bit the water. What are you using?

swam in their heads. What are you using. Using? They leaned forward where the water sunk deep to shadows. They looked past the mirror of their faces, down past the first tips of weeds, down again to where the water swirled once beyond a red rock pocked by the turning current, down to where White Crow danced dead in the water. Her eyes were dark and open, looking up from green darkness, looking up to see them all looking down on her, lost to water, White Crow, her long hair a tangle of weeds.

The white man pulled the rings from his fingers, the coins from his deep pockets, and tossed them onto the hard ground. Gleaming. The Indian men could hear the high, tinny sounds of silver dollars bouncing off rocks, a hundred small lights they could see from the corners of their eyes falling to darkness.

And when the Indian men pulled White Crow up from water, their hearts split with tears to see the open wound of her, the openness of her flesh fluttering to the open mouths of fish. White Crow slit from her woman hole to the hollow of her throat, her lungs now ghostly fish, her warm heart nibbled and cold.

Then these men, these Indians, they did back to the white man what the white man had done, not thinking of what it might do to them, not thinking what more it would take. These Indians, they beat the white man hard with river rocks until his breath stopped. They took all the things he wore on his body. They took his shiny black boots, even a picture in his pocket of a small-eyed white woman. They beat the teeth from his gums with a wedge rock and dropped his long-rooted teeth in their pockets. Then they did to the white man what he had done to White Crow. They put a knife up the hole of his ass. They slit him up between his balls. They held their breath while they slit the pocket of his stomach and broke the pee sack. The Indians took the white man's white horse and painted it red with his blood. Then these Indians held the white man up above their heads and shoved the muzzle of the horse into the white man's hollow torso like a death mask, bound his body round the horse's head and neck with tight thongs. The blind animal's nostrils quivered with the scent of its owner's blood.

Then these Indians sent the horse back as far as he could make it to the white man's camp. But the horse stood still and when they slapped its haunches, the shied horse bolted, caught up in tall river bramble, the naked ass of the white man splayed over the horse's neck, the white man's arms and legs beating the sides of the struggling horse. And when the horse fell, it couldn't toss its head to get back up for the weight of the white man. And when the horse died and the white man and the horse began to bloat and stink by the river, the other Indians broke camp and tried to leave the smell and the bad feeling. But they couldn't get far enough away from the stink so locked on the land they were. Even though they wept for White Crow, the white man, and the pitiful horse, they couldn't escape what these Indian men had done nor what the white man had started. Not even after these Indian men had buried the white man and his horse, not even after the other white men came looking and could not find the white man or his horse or even catch the dry whiff of his white bones, the stench of the horse's blue gases, the bad smell, followed the tribe.

These Indians, they brought some bad things here a long time ago. They brought the ghost of a white man to us because they gave him a place to shit his bad desires. And we must remember that something has gone wrong with us, something has made us scared of ourselves and what we know. Something has made us step back from the water and hold our shaking sides. We have lost ourselves when we let the white man come too close, when we give ourselves away. And we need to go back to the water first, to listen, to embrace the ghosts that shiver our bellies. And sometimes when we are fishing in the smooth lakes in slow circles, when in the greenest currents the fat pike leap from the water with snapping teeth at dusk and the sky overhead is still and clear and the fish are blind, we are close to White Crow, her blood puffing clouds in the deep water, calling us. And there is a bad smell here sometimes coming up from the rivers and streams when we are deep in our dreams of big fish beneath our boats opening their mouths to our hooks. A bad smell we should not ignore, like the musk smell of a deer that has died without prayer. Because little by little, over all these many years, the power is still leaving us, and we have to hook it, snag it like a great struggling fish and pull it back.

Winter Deeds

Don't ask me why I agreed to do it or why I did it. I've been asking myself the same damn question now for at least three days. It was money. I was drunk. The way I see it, I did both of them a favor. Stoner and the man near Charlo. But it scared me. I got spooked again, real good this time. I felt something strange standing out there in that man's field. I kept touching the crotch of my pants like I'd pissed myself when I hadn't. At one point I remember looking up at the moon and it was so bright, but only on me, as if anyone looking out in the black fields could see me like one big asshole standing in a hard light. In the moonlight I could count the buttons on my coat. I could see the wart on my left hand and the twist-skin where the rope had almost burned my thumb off when I was fifteen. The halter buckle was shining silver, so bright I had to squint my eyes. I was drunk enough to say hell with it, to get back in my truck and drive the hell away from there, to drive past Pretty Chief's house and yell for him to come out.

I went there to this stranger's house like Stoner had asked me to with every intention of killing that quarter horse, of stringing it up on the man's porch like a used gunnysack. Chop a hindquarter for chops for the dog. I don't know what I had to be afraid of. I'd seen a hundred horses killed, maybe more. Too old to be living, lame, sway-backed, broken-down nags. And hell, here I spent an hour getting ready like I was stalking, like I didn't know the horse was kept in a steal-easy corral close to the house on good nights and in the third stall over from the Dutch barn doors on winter nights like we been having. You tell yourself things, things you don't want to hear when your heart goes sour and you're walking too fast toward trouble. But I was bad that night, standing at the corner of this stranger's house, smoking. He had a few horses, not much, but I knew I was hearing the horse I was going to be killing. Those horses know. I heard his box kick in the stall, straight out, not hard but nervous, testing, ready to run. He could smell my blood, the noose in my hand, the blade of my iron knife. I was getting a little cold waiting but I thought I should wait even though there was nothing going on in the house. The man was sleeping or else he could be waiting at a black window with a power scope, an elk rifle that could split a man. I took my chances like a cowboy. I stepped out from the house. I listened to my footprints, the puff of my breath. I looked behind me but the house was still. The son of a bitch didn't sleep like any rancher I knew. I smiled to myself. Hell, once this was over I could kick back for a whole hard season. I could hire me a ranch hand to boss around. I could screw Louise maybe in a fine hotel in Missoula. I'd smoke a good cigar while warming my ass in a tub full of hot soapy water. I'd squeeze me some big tits, have a real good time. With money like this I would hammer the thick heads of a hundred head of cattle.

The barn door was open a ways. I walked in like I owned the place. I made small noises deep in my throat and puffed out my breath in deep heaves, trying to give this horse my scent. I pulled out my lighter and lit the darkness for a short while. I could see the nostrils of the other horses first, then their huge, quiet eyes, open wide to me, their ears starched. I walked carefully past them. I reached in my pocket for small bits of sweet apple. They sniffed but would not taste. I saw the quarter horse, not in the third stall but in the very last stall over. He stood calm-eyed and quiet in his stall, alert and powerful. I lifted up my lighter and he backed off. I could see the deep muscles in the horse's shoulders, the withers defined by light, the rump was like a driving force, a mass of engine in horse flesh. I grabbed the jaw, a cutting horse, a good one. I was glad I didn't bring my special choke bit. The horse was trusting. I slipped the halter over its Roman head. I snapped the lighter and looked at this horse again. I had wanted a horse like this since my father first made me ride his hell mare. A mare, not a stallion, that threw me from her back three times and knocked me off against the corner of the corral, running a dead heat so hard that she spun off my kneecap.

This horse was obedient. Still, I was the son of a bitch that could kill him. I felt the edge of my knife through its leather holster. I walked him on out past the barn, out back to the fields. I could see him. I didn't talk to the horse like I do. I reached under its barreled throat and felt for a strong pulse of blood. The blood surged through the horse, a heat I could feel like power near the base. Some asshole told me once to slit the tongue of a big animal like a snake's tongue so the blood will choke the sound of killing, or just slit the tongue and rope the mouth, have a cup of coffee and come back in an hour. Done. I thought. I looked down the horse's mouth. A stupid idea from too many bar belts. I put my hand down on the great chest of the horse and decided to stab him hard, three times. Slug him. The blade deep. Drop him. I stepped back to take off my coat, and the back of the horse quivered. "Just do it," I said to myself. I reached into my pocket and took out the leather sheath. I put it between my legs to hold on to it and took off my coat. "Just do it, you son of a bitch." I could hear the pull of the knife through leather. I was ready. I gritted my teeth. I grabbed the halter and pulled the horse close to me. I could smell the sweet sweat of its mane. I had the reins in my fist and the horse's head up when I felt a breath on my back so hot I wondered if my skin was already freezing. I turned to look behind me and I saw nothing. Nothing at all.

I positioned the point of my blade to the horse's big chest. I pumped my arm and lifted it far back, behind me. I thrust down with all the power in the sleeve of my arm, with all the muscles in my back. I wheezed in the struggle of my own strength but something happened. My arm didn't move. My arm didn't move one inch and I looked behind me and there it was, still suspended in air, ready to go. "You are a drunk son of a bitch," I said to myself. But my arm wouldn't move. It hung there almost for the longest time. And I turned and had me a real good look in the dark. And for one crazy moment I could've sworn I saw something, something like a ghost, standing just beyond me, but I couldn't see much. What I really saw was bones, blue bones. I could count ribs like a fat coil that was busted down the center and had lifted up. I could see a man's ribs. I could see the thighbones. And I wasn't spooked just then. If anything, I was dry sober. I was standing cold in a dry wind in snow, dry sober, looking at a ghost that should have been a sight for drunkenness but I was sober. It was the ghost of a man. I knew that, the way you know for no reason at all, that someone is watching you from behind. I wasn't afraid. I loaded that horse up in the back of my rig and drove on out to Whiskey Flats. I let that horse go on five thousand acres of raw land, not knowing why, just knowing that was the thing to do at the time. I saw the spray of its tail, lifted high, beautiful, as he headed out. I didn't worry about the winter. I didn't worry about the drop of the thermometer on bad nights, the slick rocks, the bad drops. I let that horse go free. I turned it loose on a night so cold I saw the blue bones of a ghost. And I didn't care about Stoner just then. I could make up a story. I could just say the farmer came out when I was ready to drop his horse so I took the horse and ran. I could tell him I dropped the horse, one shot in the Whiskey Hills. But that son of a bitch, I know he'll be thinking, just like I'd think myself, that I took the horse for me but even if I did, he'd owe me. He'll owe me big for this one.

I got Roy Hearn to wake up in the middle of the night. I pounded at his window so the lazy son of a bitch would get up before daylight. He didn't even ask me what I was doing on his porch at two in the morning. He sold me one of his glue horses, pick any one, he said. And I went out back and felt guilty as hell to look at all these broken-down horses, scarred, some limping, waiting for the truck to take them into Bozeman. No longer horses, no longer good rides or a cowboy's freedom. Now they were meat.

I found one the same color as the farmer's horse, the same color. I put that horse down right there. Roy yelled out his window once at me. "Trying to sleep," he said. But the horse had already gone to rest. I skinned it right there with the other horses huddled against the farthest fence. Hell, they know what's going on. I held my nose. The whiskey was still in me somewhere, threatening to come back up my throat at the smell, the deep gut smell, the bad smell of death that should have come years ago. Animal death ached in my nose. I popped the knife into hard bone. Stung my fingers like a son of a bitch. I drained some blood into a water pouch I kept behind my seat. When I had gutted the horse, I pulled the hide away from the corral. I left the meat still steaming. I figured Roy would appreciate the extra meat for no money. I got in my truck and turned to look at the corral. Smoke rose up from the shivering horses' backs and I thought to myself they'd be steaming like the other horse, but only in a butcher's concrete room in a few days and maybe I'd done this one horse a favor. But I'm a son of a bitch. I don't need a dozen doe-eyed horses flinching back from me to tell me. I know I'm a son of a bitch.

By the time I got to the first curve in the road to Charlo, I had to pull over my truck and lose the whiskey. I could feel the chafe of whiskers on my collar. I saw the farmer's house again. I got out of the truck and lowered the tailgate. A powder of snow covered the horse hide. I put my gloves on and opened the hide out flat and a heavy heat rose from it. A bitter smoke. There was a feeling of morning rising in the air. The colors were flat. The mountains were edged now. The stars were thinning.

I looked at the man's house in the distance. He had slept through this long assault. He was still snoring. A sorry son of a bitch. I reached into the truck and picked up the water bag. I slung the horse hide on my back and my bad knee bowed. My boots crunched the field snow. I felt the cold in my battered ass, the click of my teeth. Everyone must be sleeping.

About halfway to the field, I realized what a sorry son of a bitch I really am. A crazy asshole that has chased a good man's horse to hell, lost a good night's sleep and at a minute to morning is still up, pranking like a schoolboy without a lick of brains. I had lost my heart for the job. I decided to hell with Harvey Stoner. I'm leaving the carcass on the corral. And I left. By the time I got back to my truck my knees were buckling with cold. The back of my head was tight and I looked up to see the farmer's light glowing in the distance. I rolled down my window as I was driving away, still in semi-darkness. I left my headlamps off. I stopped once, listening for an angry voice but I heard nothing but the popping of my tires over frozen road. And all the way home I could hear a crying so hard I would look into my rearview mirror to see if someone was in the truck bed behind me. But there was no one, not in the lonesome truck bed or the seat behind me. There was no one, only me.

Old Ghosts

A smiling woman picked her up about a half mile from the Vullets' house and when Louise told her that she was Indian the woman stopped talking. The woman's face was a shadow in the warm car. The woman steered her car onto the first wide spot in the road. She had reached across Louise's lap and had tugged at the door handle while the car was still moving. The woman's face was tight and for a moment Louise thought that she was smiling. The car pulled to a slow roll and stopped. The woman pushed the door out so hard the springed hinges creaked and the door came back fast at Louise. The woman drew her chin in tight to her chest and stared up at Louise. Louise got out of the car and before the woman had the door closed she was off again.

Louise watched the spin of the woman's tires on the slick roadside. The woman rode the pedal. Louise heard the high whine of the wheels grinding. The wheels spun so hard they almost burned. When the tires finally took hold, the car whiplashed down the highway for such a long way that Louise began hoping the car would right itself again.

Night was pressing hard over the hills, a charcoal face, Louise thought, the chest and front legs of a giant horse running, clouds turning. She stood at the road and looked over at the dull silver river. She could see the black water where the animals had chipped a hole in the ice. Day was sinking. Through the naked trees she heard the river's voice. Louise told herself it was only the ice, the fingernail-thin ice pulling on the shore. Louise squinted at the water skin rattling on the river, the place where the current ran hard. The still-water place where her sister had died last summer. She stood for a long time watching the spot of her sister's death hoping she could call her sister back. For a moment there was no sound. Snow snaked on the road. She watched with her eyes clear and seeing. She watched with a heart in her chest, her heart slowing. She could feel the day around her slipping. The closer you are to life, the closer you are to death, her grandmother had told her. She wondered if now was one of those times. When she heard the ice crack she felt the break along her spine, an opening. She listened to the shrill splitting river. A sound like a woman moaning crossed the water bank.

A mule deer leaped from the dense brush and clipped across the changing river. Louise heard its hollow clocking steps kicking ice and then its hooves broke to water. The ice creaked like an old door closing. She saw, not wanting to believe what it was she was seeing.

She saw the deer's dark eyes roll up white, a clear splash of water gurgling. And then the river was silent. She stood for a moment looking toward the dense call of water. This was the place where her sister must have looked up once maybe or again and again without seeing or seeing only this panic of water rising up her neck. Louise's hands trembled. She ran toward the river, not taking her eyes off the hole where the deer had broken through. Brambles scratched her face. She slipped and fell and saw the chuffing mouth of the hole, a small hiss of water smoking and the animal gone. She got back up, chased the river run from the bank, watching the still river place, her own heart strangled by the thought of water, trying to see beneath green swirls of ice, hoping she hadn't seen the deer fall through, still hoping she could save it somehow. But she knew the water ran fast here and never froze. She had never known there to be a fishing hole here in winter. Water only glazed.

The deer was gone.

The wind chattered in the red bramble.

She stopped running and felt her breath tight in her chest. How many times that summer day, Louise wondered, had her sister lifted her face up from the water only to smell this place here, the burn of nettle, the smell of sky meeting water? The last memory for Amelia must have been the sweet smells the river inhales in slow pockets that somehow turn into the length of a long summer and become the only thing we remember. A blind and blinding memory.

She pointed her steps homeward and felt the wind gather speed. It pushed at her back. She felt her nerves stinging cold. The tips of her ears itched. She began to wonder if she had ever seen the deer. She watched her feet. The snow was so cold-dry she could hear the squeak of her footsteps and a sudden quiet. The quiet that meets the day at evening. Her breath steamed in front of her. She tried to think of home. She tried to think of a warm place. She saw only the big poster bed in Stoner's house. The small pillows. The framed pictures on the walls. She could almost feel the heat rushing up the vents, heat rushing to the pulse in her throat, hot, the first glare of summer again and again, so hot she would drop her clothes and stand naked to open-mouthed Harvey Stoner just to feel the breath of the furnace. She could stand barefoot and naked on the hot brass plate, press her hand to the window, and melt ice in a winter that dipped to twenty below, and never feel the sting of cold. She would stand on the vent until the scorch of hot brass nipped the tough soles of her feet.

He would lie on the bed sometimes. He would lie on the bed and unzip his pants to touch himself, to watch her. She would hold her breasts for him. He would cry sometimes. She would drape herself in a white sheet and pretend to be his daughter. She would braid her hair. And Harvey Stoner would kiss her. She could smell cigarette smoke in the deep pores of his skin and she would pull back from him. He would kiss her hair until her hair would unwind from its braid. And he would smile and sleep. And she would sneak downstairs to visit his wife's pantry.

In the dark, in a room bigger than her grandmother's house, she would feel the full stacked shelves. She would touch the store-bought cans of peaches, plums, pears, the shelves without beans or sacks of dry meat. She could feel no mouse turds or spider webs. The room smelled like boxes of apples, Macintosh or Transparent. And while Harvey Stoner slept she would drink the juice from a cool can of apricots. She would eat his sweet peaches in the good-smelling room. And then she would walk home, leaving Harvey to find a row of empty cans lining his wife's clean kitchen counter.

Louise had never really seen Mrs. Stoner before today. In the distance she had always looked like a woman who had a lot of money. In her passing car she always looked satisfied and happy. She looked almost young. But today Louise had seen her face up close. She had seen the face of a woman who had slept with Harvey Stoner for fourteen years. Fourteen years of new cars and big rings. And she saw in the woman's face a mean sadness. Years of wondering, years of younger women, girls, really. And Louise hated Harvey Stoner. Once she had slept with another man just to get the scent of Harvey Stoner off her skin. The nights he pulled her into his car to suck her breasts were the nights she wouldn't go home. She would stay outside her grandmother's house. Now Harvey Stoner could touch her and it didn't matter anymore. She felt only small tugs on her skin, a heat on her belly, and then he was gone. And the less it bothered her, the less it mattered to her, and the more he wanted her. And the more he wanted her, the less it mattered to her. Until he became small to her. She wasn't sure what she wanted from him now. All Louise could feel was her hunger. A want that stayed with her like a small bird that chirped in her dreams, woke her hungry.

She was cold and tired. She would sit down by the roadside just for a minute, she told herself. She hugged herself and squeezed her hands beneath her arms. She blinked her eyes to the cold, to the dark coming. She sat still to the silver river and the silver-pink sky. She sat still. She sat as if her breathing had left her. The hills were turning dark against the pale sky. The flutter of birds had quieted to night. She could see the shadowy branches of the cottonwoods down by the river. She remembered the hushed noises of a hundred settled birds, then the rush of robin's wings leaving. She thought of her sister Amelia. Her sad, sweet smile. All the sweet, wild roses were gone. The huckleberries, sarvis berries, Indian celery, were long sleeping beneath the knee-deep snow. The fat deer had chased the new growth far up the timberline. And the mule deer she had seen was now cradled in the swirling river far down the river, swallowed, rocking to dark silt. The land was deep in the crushing sleep of winter. Louise blew breath into the cup of her white palms. She stuffed her hands back into her pockets and felt the tight curl of her fingers, the burn of blood. She would sit down on the roadside for just a moment, she told herself again. When she closed her eyes she could see the pale sun.

It was Jules. Jules in his blister-blue truck, his headlights smoking. He had lifted her from the roadside and carried her to his truck. He had made her mad. She had slapped him for waking her when the good dreams had just started to come. The windshield was frosted with his breath. The moonlight was white. She could smell the sweat of horses, the scratch of heavy wool at her face. Jules had thrown his horse blanket on her. She couldn't open her eyes even when she knew Jules was pounding the dashboard to wake her. The heater hummed. And she turned toward sleep.

He slapped at her face until the roots of her hair were fire. "Christ," he whispered. "Christ." There was white moonlight. The curve of the river flashing. The sleepy shift of the truck rounding curves. And Jules whispering. Whispering to the sound of the slick hum of wheels. "I'm taking you to my home, Louise. You'll be fine. I'm taking care of you," he said. "I need to go to Missoula tomorrow early. But I'll be back. I'll be back," he said. She thought he had kissed her hair. And she remembered that he had carried her into a dark house that smelled like camphor and tobacco. He had taken off her clothes, jerked her arms out of her sleeves. She opened her eyes to see his sleek chest, to see him naked and pulling back the blankets on his bed. She remembered the heavy pull of sleep again, the blankets, the thick heat of Jules's hands cupping her buttocks, the way her teeth chattered even in sleep.

"Jesus," he said. "You could have died out there."

She heard him in the morning as he was leaving but he did not say goodbye. She lifted the curtain and saw the dark light of dawn. She pulled the covers back up and closed her eyes. She thought she was alone.

The woman was in the kitchen and Louise watched her lift her hand above her eyes as if she were squinting into the bright sunlight or as if she were waiting, watching for someone. Louise knew that she was in the house of Jules Bart. She remembered the rooms. She could see his work pants on the floor of the kitchen, a pair of long underwear over a chair. The woman walked carefully to the cookstove and opened the door without gloves. The fire was so hot, Louise could feel it from where she stood but when she walked closer the kitchen was cool. She could place her hand in the stove even though she could still hear the crack of the hot wood fire. The kettle hissed on the stove without steam.

The woman was dressed in a long skirt. Her hair was brown, light brown, and over her ears was a fresh spray of bluest lupine. The woman looked out the window and wiped her hands on her apron. Someone was coming. Louise looked outside. The snow was falling and she wondered if she might be dreaming.

Louise walked barefoot into the living room. She could hear

birds outside, hundreds of birds, and yet she knew it was winter. She listened closely. From the far field she could hear the mourning dove and meadowlark. She opened up the door to hear better. She opened up the door to see summer, and an ice-tingling wind shot through the house and slammed all the doors shut.

Louise turned to the woman. "Hello," Louise said to the strange woman, "hello." The woman did not answer her. It was as if the woman did not see Louise at all and when Louise stepped into the kitchen she felt cold. Her teeth chattered and her shoulders ached from shaking.

Louise turned to see the woman throw a shawl over her shoulders. She was clear as water now. The hair of a ghost, the pale eyes of a ghost turning to Louise. Louise could see death now turning to pass through the door of Jules Bart's house. Louise could feel the cold lifting from the woman like heat lifts from the road in hottest summer. Nothing. And beyond her leaving, in the dream of the smallest second, the pale, green grass of a spring morning. Buttercups and buds.

Louise found her pants and her shirt in the bedroom. She found a pair of dirty socks that weren't hers and decided to put them on anyway. She grabbed her boots and dressed as she moved to the door. She knew she had to get home, that her grandmother would be worried about her. She slid her stocking feet on the floor of the dining room. She bent over to tie her boots and heard someone. She heard someone talking. It sounded like a young man with a cracking voice. She was hoping it was Jules.

Louise does not want to see them but she sees them. She puts her chin to her chest and prays that she is dreaming. When Louise looks up she sees the woman again. This time the woman is unmoving. This time Louise knows the woman is dead. She is laid out on the dining room table. She is shoeless. Her toenails are long and yellow. Louise holds still.

A young man, a boy, really, enters the room with a steaming bowl of water. He looks like Jules but he is only fourteen years old at most. He sets the bowl down and Louise gets a sudden whiff of spearmint. He has scented the water. The smell makes Louise lonesome for summer and she remembers the warm smell of sweet grass above the river.

The woman is still on the table. Louise looks at the woman's dress, the long folds that drape to the floor. It is a heavy dress. The woman's hair is in a tight knot at the top of her head. Her face has been wind-beaten smooth. The young man takes the pins from her hair one by one and her hair untwists from her head and touches the floor. Her hair is brown and silver and the boy brushes her hair carefully. She can hear the whistle of his breath through clenched teeth. He brushes her hair for a long time, smoothing each brush stroke with his hand. Louise feels a tightness in her chest. Even though it is winter she can hear the quaking aspens outside shivering silver. Louise hears the warm wind. She wonders if she steps outside if she can hold this time.

He washes his hands for a long time and then he carefully unbuttons the woman's dress. There are many buttons but he takes his time. His hands shine at her throat. There is a quiet in the room made quieter by his breathing. He unbuttons every button, unsnaps every snap, and when he is finished he struggles to remove the dress from her. He props her left elbow, trying to yank the sleeve. He doesn't cry. He seems angry now and he tears the dress up the left sleeve and bares her arm. He tears the dress again, exposing both of her thick arms. He dips a washcloth in the steaming water. He hisses. The water is hot. Louise can smell spearmint. He lifts the woman's wrist and swipes her arm twice. The boy takes a long breath. The woman is heavy on the table in her long skirt and bodice. She has more clothes on than the living. Louise knows the boy will undress her.

He starts with the bodice. He unlaces it. Louise hears the slap of the laces unthreaded. Her body opens slowly as if she has been bound tight all of her life. The woman's breasts blossom. They are large and white. The boy doesn't look at them. His hands are long and slender. He tries to undo her slip. He walks to the end of the table and tugs at the hem of the slip, trying to pull it off her. Her body moves down the table a bit. He jerks again and when he looks up to see her breasts jiggling he stops his effort. His neck is red and his face looks hot. He stands for a moment. He looks at the woman's face and then he digs in his pocket. He pulls out a small closed knife. He opens the blade with his teeth and slits her skirt open. By the time he gets to her full hips he realizes she is naked. He realizes he has passed the cuff of his hand through the hair between her legs. Louise closes her eyes for a moment, knowing she is seeing something that she should not be seeing. He pulls a breath so tight into his chest and stumbles back so fast Louise knows he has touched the woman in a private way. He backs up for a moment. He looks at the floor. He looks at the door.

Louise thinks that he is finished. She feels that he will leave this task. But he goes back to the woman. He strains the hot cloth in his fist without wincing. He washes her face. He places the cloth to her breast like he's not touching her at first. And then he is washing her hard. He is washing her like a table. And he cries. He puts his head down on her chest and he cries hard. Louise realizes he is alone. There is no one for him. He cries so hard the table shakes. He sucks at the woman a little, then he sucks her breast hard. Louise bites her lip, surprised at how she feels, how his sadness grips her chest. He cries open-mouthed at the ceiling. He puts his head back down on the woman's chest. His mother, Louise thinks, feeling stupid for not knowing that from the beginning. His dead mother. He stops crying for a while. He looks up straight at Louise and she sees the young face of Jules Bart. She wants to hide from him but she knows he cannot see her. Jules Bart looks up like he realizes he is not alone. He has been seen.

And then the man comes in. He has seen Jules. He has seen Jules at his mother's breast crying. He is pulling the gloves from his hands. Jules Bart kneels down and covers his head and all Louise hears is the sound of the man's dull fists on the backs of Jules's hands, his arms, his hollow chest.

Seed

1.

He looked at the seed for a long time.
His mind did not comprehend.
It did not flower anymore.
The seed was just a seed.

                          She had said it was begonia.
He tried to imagine what begonias looked like.
Purple blossoms, rich yellow, supple orange, blue petals?

The mind that made the seed bloom was always the poet.

He was not the poet anymore.

2.

When he decided to give up poetry,
it was one o'clock in the afternoon.
It was a Tuesday, and he stood in the middle of a corridor
trying to think of where to go, where he was to be.
Where? he wondered. Mighty big question, he decided.
He knew then he would quit trying to write poetry,
the seed he thought he carried with him all his life.
Here he was at forty-five years old still trying
to show he was the one who would show
such life in images no one could deny.

There were no images.
He watched his graduate seminar students stumbling
into H-103 every Tuesday afternoon.
The Grim Section, they called it, Richard's class,

the one with the dark side of Tennyson.
Tennyson had no major dark side, not a grim one anyway,
but he brought it out. He made sure of it.
                              It wasn't true, but he made it true.
There were no such images, he thought.

So at one o'clock on a Tuesday afternoon,
Richard decided, No more.
He didn't say anything to the blond female student
walking straight up to him as he turned away.
He could have walked through walls, ether walls
and star-sheened walls and even solid walls,
when he left Hallmer Hall without looking back.

3.

When he reached First Elk River,
the stream of water was not like any he had ever stood by.
Not even the one he had created when his parents,
professors, and wives had said, You are the gentlest,
subtlest, most sincere one.
                              Sure he took advantage
of the Buddha when he said, Why not.
                              And laughed,
and they smiled and said to others, That's what he says.

Now, by First Elk River all he could see were reeds
and the water flowing.
Unsteadily, he was the angle of water turning.
And he remembered one of his lectures at the beginning
of the semester when he had brought up a Chinese poet
who observed that nothing turns without meaning to.
Unsteadily, he was turning but now he was meaning to turn.

4.

There was a story he liked that no one else remembered.
It was a funeral story by an Irish writer, he was sure.

Maybe the writer who wrote *A Tree Grows in Brooklyn*.
Someone who had said, "No one ever sees the river anymore."
Maybe he made that up; he couldn't remember either
anymore.

They had not forgotten but it was best to forget,
so they forgot.
        But the fishing they didn't forget;
at least the memory of fishing they didn't forget.
So he remembered the flowing current as he watched
the trout swim deftly through the current shifting always.

He did not want to be a poet anymore.
He did not want to be swayed by the lilt of a bird somewhere
beyond his view as he reached his hand toward the current
shifting everything away, and he did not want to know
the seed that stood before his eyes as a tiny monument
of new life, the beginning that would flower by his seeing.

Believe This

There was a time
I wanted nothing so much as home.
In the rain I loved you, in the hot days;
The corn ripened; I was a child of storms
And of seasons.
I ventured and was lost,
But, oh, those salty songs of the damned!
Death has a green foot,
And we dance like fools.

Flight

John-John had been saving dollar bills toward a dream and when he had a shoebox full of bills he sat down to count out his future. "One, two, three," he counted, all the way up to ten to make a neat stack on the floor and soon, he had two hundred neat stacks in exact rows and columns.

How much is enough?

John-John packed a suitcase with his dollar bills, a change of underwear, a toothbrush, and a photograph of his older brother, Joseph. The photograph was folded, spindled, mutilated. Joseph, the jet pilot, sat in full military dress in front of an American flag.

Dear Mr. and Mrs. _____, we regret to inform you that your son, _____, was shot down and taken prisoner by the enemy during a routine military operation. At this time, we are doing everything within our power to assure the immediate and safe release of your son.

Sincerely, they said.

John-John remembered the world before, remembered the four walls and one window of the HUD house on the reservation. So, most Indians had no job and they counted change to buy the next bottle of wine. Maybe the wells went dry every summer and maybe any water still left was too radioactive to drink.

"Uranium has a half-life of one hundred thirty-five million years," somebody told Joseph, and he said, "Shit, I can tell you stories that will last longer than that."

Then, there was music.

Joseph sang in a voice so pure even the drunkest Indians threw their bottles down. He sang in a voice so sharp even the oldest Indians could hear him clearly. He sang in a voice so deep even the whitest Indians remembered the words.

Sometimes, he danced.

Joseph had big feet and he stumbled, often lost the rhythm of drums. But he smiled and picked himself up from the ground after he fell. He whistled. He slapped his thighs. He crow-hopped and sprained his ankle. He danced.

Joseph paid the rent.

After Joseph was taken prisoner of war, John-John waited at the window for years. He ate and drank at that window; he slept with his eyes open. John-John's friends grew up, graduated or dropped out of school, married, had children, got drunk too much, but he stood there at the window and waited.

John-John remembered: the sky and ground disappeared into the horizon, that imaginary line forever rolling away. Snow. Ice. Cold wind. Joseph in blue parka and military surplus boots. After Christmas but before New Year's Eve. Everyone was sober. Standing in some anonymous field while his Chevy sat a few feet away on the other side of a fence, Joseph raised his arms and said, *Someday, the world will be mine.* Maybe he just said, *Goddamn, I need a drink.* Joseph had already dug through the ashtray, in the glove compartment, under seats. There was no money left in the world. Not even loose coins. *We ain't got gas and I'm out of miracles,* Joseph said and walked fifteen miles for help.

Now, John-John stood on the front porch with his suitcase, a key hanging on a string around his neck. No lock, no door. The key was just a small mystery. It didn't fit any lock on the reservation. Maybe it opened a garage door in Seattle; maybe it started a car in Spokane.

John-John watched the sky for signs, read the sun for the correct time, and checked his watch to be sure. *It's time to go,* he thought just as the jet ripped through the sound barrier and shook the air. John-John tumbled down the stairs, landed on his tailbone. He stood up, rubbed his ass, and searched the sky for evidence. He could see vapor trails stretched across the sky.

John-John ran for the football field, down the reservation highway, three miles of smooth, smooth pavement. It happens that way: the tribe had a government grant to fix the roads but half the Indians on the reservation still lived on commodities. But John-John ran until his chest hurt and legs trembled. He ran to the ends of the highway and stared back toward his house, at the jet approaching, then landing with a concussion of noise.

The jet taxied down the highway, turbines slowing, and came to a stop a few feet from John-John. Power. Heat. Noise. It all felt and sounded like possibilities; it was the machinery of dreams. John-John stared at the jet until it grew beyond his vision. His eyes watered, ached. He rubbed at them with fists until they grew out of proportion. Minutes went by until the jet was silent in the silence its arrival created.

Has Christopher Columbus come back?

John-John walked toward the jet, slowly, carefully. His steps were measured and precise. Step on a crack, break your mother's back. A balance beam is only four inches wide; the reservation is only half that width. John-John reached out and touched the jet with a fingertip. Hot and cold. He jumped back as the cockpit opened and a voice called out.

"Sir, ace jet pilot Joseph Victor, code name Geronimo, reporting for duty, sir!"

A tall man climbed down from the cockpit and stood at attention. His unbraided hair fell out from under his flight helmet, reached down to the small of his back. The tall man saluted John-John then wheeled and saluted the crowd of Indians quickly gathering. He turned back to John-John.

"Sir, may I have permission to remove my helmet, sir?"

John-John was stunned. He raised his arm in a half-salute, the heels of his tennis shoes clicked together.

"Joseph, is that you?"

"Sir, yes, sir. May I please remove my helmet, sir?"

"Yeah, go ahead."

Joseph removed his helmet, leaned it against a hip, still at attention. His face was scarred, battered. The purple scar between his eyes was shaped like a cigar butt; the symmetrical scars up and down his cheeks looked like gills.

"Joseph, your face. What happened?"

John-John moved closer to his brother, reached out and touched the scars, the skin. Hot and cold. Both close to tears.

"Sir, it's been a long and glorious war but I am happy to be home, sir."

"But, your face. What did they do to you?"

"Sir, I am proud to say I withstood their tortures with courage and strength. I only gave them my name, rank, and serial number, sir."

John-John cried then, took his brother's hand. Swollen and scratched, Joseph's hand felt like fear and failure. He had lost his left ring finger, his nails were torn, some missing altogether. Crude initials were carved into his palms.

"Joseph, don't you recognize me? It's your brother, John-John."

Joseph stared at his brother intently, searched his memory. He saw those eyes curved like a bow, colored like the center of the earth; that hair short and still untamed, black; that mouth, too small for the face, those teeth yellowed and healthy; those hands, that hand now holding his, so long and forgiving, skin like a woman's.

Who are you? Who are you?

"Sir, I don't remember. I'm sorry. I just don't remember, sir."

Memory, like a coin trick, like the French drop with one hand passing over the other, quarter dropping into sight, then out of existence. *It was there! It was there!* The little Indian boys screaming at the sudden recognition of their first metaphor. Memory like an abandoned car, rusting and forgotten though it sits in plain view for decades. Dogs have litters there; generations of spiders live a terrible history. All of it goes unnoticed and no one bothers to tell the story.

This is not the story John-John tells himself just before he falls asleep. In his story, Joseph comes back on a bus, on a train, hitchhiking. In his story, Joseph's feet never leave the ground again. But that kind of vision is costly; it rips sweat from John-John's sleep and skin. He wakes up with a thirst so large that nothing can be forgiven. He wakes up with the sound of Joseph's voice in his nose. Reverberation.

"Hey, John-John, why do you got two first names?"

"Cuz you have to say anything twice to make it true?"

"No, that ain't it."

"Cuz our parents really meant it when they named me?"

"I don't think so."

"Maybe it's just a memory device."

"Who knows?"

Joseph sitting at the kitchen table as they replay this conversation, this way of greeting, each day. Ever since John-John could form a sentence, Joseph began the morning with the same question.

"Hey, John-John, why do you got two first names?"

"Cuz I'm supposed to be twins?"

"No, man, that's too easy."

"Cuz mother always had a stutter?"

Laughter. Then, more laughter. Then, coffee and buttered toast. Sometimes, a day-old donut. The sun came in through the windows. It was there, just as much as the tablecloth or the salt and pepper shakers.

Hey, John-John, why do you got two first names?

Now, John-John waiting at the window. Watching. Telling the glass his stories, whispering to the pane, his breath fogging the world. His house, his family's house, closed in all around him. Too many photographs. Too many stray papers and tattered magazines. The carpet has fleas.

There have been smaller disasters.

Mother and father, sister and sister, rush, rush. Fumigate, bleach and vinegar in the laundry, old blankets driven to the dump. The dog, lonely and confused, chained to a spare tire in the yard.

"John-John," his mother says. "You have to leave. I mean, we all have to leave the house for a few hours. It'll be toxic for a while, you know?"

He is dragged from the window, sat down beside the dog on the lawn. They both howl.

Once, John-John dreamed of flight. He imagined a crazed run into the forest, into the pine. Maybe then they would search for him, search for Joseph out there in the dark. John-John wanted to build fires with no flame or smoke. He wanted to hide in the brush while searchers walked by, inches away, calling out his name. He wanted helicopters with spotlights, all-terrain vehicles, the local news. Together, they would lift stones and find Joseph; they would shake trees and Joseph would fall to the ground; they would drink Joseph from their canteens; they would take photographs of Joseph crawling like a bear across snow, stunned by winter. The rescue team would find John-John and Joseph huddled together like old men, like children, like small birds tensing their bodies for flight.

John-John sits at his window. Waits. Watches. His face touches the glass. Hot and cold. His eyes follow the vapor trails that appear in the reservation sky. They are ordinary and magical.

Next time, John-John thinks. *Next time, it will be Joseph.*

Maybe it is winter again. Maybe it is just summer disguised. There is no one left to notice. Dust. Cold wind. Noise. John-John hears it all in his head. He counts his dollar bills, *one, two three*, all the way up to ten before he starts again. He waits; he watches.

He wants to escape.

Drum as Love, Fear, and Prayer

for Diane

1.

Dance, she said.
She said, Dance.

It is crazy, I know, how quickly I've learned to love
this dancing, this step-step across the floor

when I'd spent my whole life
without any music. I had promised never to dance

in the white way
if I didn't dance in the Indian way first

but she said dance
refuses color when we are broken down

but embraces color when we are built again
and I believed her

and danced when I heard those drums, those drums
those drums in her voice.

2.

Drums
make everyone feel
like an Indian.

Drums make
everyone feel
like an Indian.

Drums make everyone
feel
like an Indian.

Drums make everyone feel
like an Indian.

Drums make everyone feel like
an Indian.

Drums make everyone feel like an Indian.

3.

And if I choose to love
this Indian woman
partly because she's Indian

(drum)

and if I choose to love
this Indian woman
mostly because she's Indian

(drum)

then who are you to stop
this love between
an Indian man and woman

(drum)

and who am I, who is she, now
for both of us to make these decisions together?

4.

I have more faith
in drums

than I have in the people
who play them

I told her
and she said God

is a drum.
I have more faith

in a small drum
because I can carry it

everywhere I go
I told her

and she said God
is the smallest drum.

5.

If love is taken
in its smallest part

will there still be enough
to frighten me? Yes

and no. I mean, if love can be
reduced to a cut bead
then I am not afraid.
But if that cut bead is sewn

into a moccasin or purse, if
that bead is part of a chain

built larger and larger, bead
by bead, then I am afraid.

Here, she said, take this bead
with honor. Then she offered another.

6.

I have broken
bread with her.

We have prayed together in silent places
where we could hear each other breathe
and in airports and lunchtime restaurants
where nothing wanted to rise above it all

except a few lonely people
and their cigarette smoke.

These prayers have not been easy, how
do we say Indian prayers in American
and which God will answer? Is God red
or white? Do these confused prayers mean

we'll live on another reservation
in that country called Heaven?

7.

She danced alone
before she ever knew me

and she'll dance alone
though she loves me

but for now
she dances

with me.
I take her hand.

No.
I take her face

in my hands
and I tell her

how much I believe
in her, in her.

8.

Then she tells me Jesus is
still here
because Jesus was
once here

and parts of Jesus are
still floating in the air.
She tells me that Jesus' DNA is
part of the collective DNA.

She tells me we are all part
of Jesus, we are all Jesus
in part. She tells me to breathe deep
during all of our storms

because you can sometimes taste Jesus
in a good hard rain.

9.

If then, we find each other
in this good way, can we say

I would have loved you
seven generations ago? No.

Can we say we couldn't have loved
another if we had never met, that

we could only love each other? No.
We can say that we love each other

now, and we can keep on loving
in this world that loves

to hurt us. Sweetheart, we can
promise never to hurt each other

and we can break and keep that promise
and we can break and keep that promise.

10.

And I want to say this (say it)
and I want to whisper (shout)
and I want to shake the doors of the house (church)
and I want to blow a trumpet (play a drum)

and I want to run (dance)
and I want to talk about laughter (pain)
and I want to count up all the loss (magic)
and I want to blow a trumpet (play a drum)

and I want to inventory my fears (joy)
and I want to hide beneath old blankets (grace)
and I want to eat too much food (faith)
and I want to blow a trumpet (play a drum)

and I want, I want, I want
to play a drum, play a drum, play a drum.

11.

Finally, the ring on your finger and isn't it somehow
strange and wonderful how much faith we have

in metaphor? Maybe I should have offered stolen horses
in exchange for your love, or a thousand eagle feathers

with a story attached to each, or given you a drum
stretched tightly with the skin of some animal I killed

and honored simultaneously. But I've never stolen anything
let alone horses, and I've never been lucky enough to find

a single eagle feather, and I've never pulled the trigger
of any gun. So what do I have left to give you? The Cross

the Star of David, a piece of the Berlin Wall? All of it
has beautiful, common meaning, but I want to be specific.

All I have to give you is this ring, which is not Indian
in its beginnings, but which can become Indian in ours.

Ponies Gathering in the Dark

The house was a forest remembering itself. The pine trees that held up the walls dreamed of stars dwelling in their needles. Jointed, branched, rooted, the trees still listened to the wind. The oak floors gleamed from the generations of human oils, but they still grew into their immense lineage of light and matter. The air between the ancient trees whispered with spirit bees and dark small birds.

Even the iron that pierced the flesh of trees had a voice. It was deep, metallic, and sank heavily in the human dreams. At night, the iron spoke most eloquently, recognizing the kinship of darkness in sky and earth. The nails sang of geodes in the heart and the gathering of elemental forces only vaguely understood. When the iron sang, humans slept, troubled, their hands remembering the first iron. The spear, the knife, the sharp edge of death.

Under the house, the ancient continent measured the journey of clay animals: giant beaver, tiny horses, elk, intricately scaled snakes, vast bears that had clawed the horizon to shreds. There is the memory of ice animals walking into the sun, their bones crushed under the weight of frozen moons. And there is the tribe of obsidian, those sharp-headed old ones, who danced around fire, singing the hunt before iron.

Long ago, the beavers built their lodges here, when the marshes were thick with mud and sweet rushes. In the middle of winter, the oldest would tell about First Beavers, giant creatures that gnawed down trees the size of the night.

The marsh became meadow; wild horses ran into the thunder of their song. They pulled grass with their strong teeth and fertilized the young pines. Their foals stood weak-kneed under the slivers of moon that spiked the trees' hearts. The horses rode the back of life and their bones crumbled into the afterbirth.

A family of black bears lived in the hollow tree that fell from the sky. A female bear shaman growled healing ceremonies, cleansing the air with broken cedar and chanting the fire back into lightning.

Later, a medicine man walked into the forest of tall trees. He heard the spirit horses drumming their hooves in the earth. All the others of their tribe, those descendants of runaway thunder, would within a short time be rounded up, branded with hot iron, put to the rein, plow, or wagon. Now, he only felt their leaving, south to hills of thick grass, and not their destiny. Only the deep belly breathing of the night horses brought out the clover smell of stars and taught the medicine man where to put his sweat lodge.

He circled a spot that spoke to him with the smooth tones of water and the rootlike dreams of animals. He cleared the brush, pulling up the grass with his strong old hands. He carried rocks which had once been polished by glacier and flood and then buried under gravel and sand. These round, rock ones danced themselves up to the rain again. Their tribe has two hundred thousand million words for themselves. And even though they have been born speckled, crystallized, pitted, brittle, they know they are still part of Grandmother Earth's medicine bag.

He carried these rocks to the fire pit. He cut down saplings and bent them down to the earth again, building a hut dark as the womb. The branches rooted into the spiritual earth. He made a fire and the rocks told the story of their molten beginnings and the wood danced away into the feathered wind. The rocks blackened and cracked, hissed and cooled, as he tossed barkfuls of water on them. Steam rose, hot and thick.

The medicine man was old. It was his last sweat. His arms were well-muscled, but his skin draped over his bones. That afternoon, he sweated where horses once snorted at coming storms.

He heard the slap of beaver tails. He felt an icy wind and saw a wavering image of a face. It was an old woman wrapped in long-furred hides. She wore a necklace of a single mammoth tooth. She smiled at him and then was gone. In the dark, what he saw was inside of him but came from beyond. He felt the bears snuffling muzzles. He nursed at one fingerlike breast.

Hours later, he crawled out of the sweat lodge. The night was clear. He sensed some kind of structure all around him. The stars shone through a roof high as the trees. It was a house, he figured out, but whether it was a metaphor for the universe or something from the future, he didn't know. The house was filled with busy humans. The people breathed their moisture into the trees. They offered up their breaths and the branches leafed out into air. People had been born in the house, their umbilical cords stretched from the salty waters to the nodding trees with their embracing branches. Cradled in wood, they slept with wood at the top of their heads where the soul enters, to the bottom of their feet, which is also called sole, but meant for grounding. The forest rose pine-scented and the people slept until they opened the thick-planked door of their death.

But what astonished him most of all was that he knew they were his children. Their skins were pink, white, brown, golden. Their eyes were the color of rocks: jade, obsidian, slate, amber. Or else the color of trees: green, yellow, brown. Some even had eyes the color of sky, water, or thunder. And their hair was the color of iron, bear, fire.

He saw them playing, laughing, arguing. He watched them dreaming, the soft dust of meteors sifting down through the roof to cover their faces with cool fire, their calm hands luminous, reaching out.

He awoke with a start. He saw the last of his vision dissolve into the cold morning air. But it had been a twisted and spotted arm that had reached out from his dreams. It was an arm from reality. His people were dying. That was why he was here, to find a way into the heart of a plant, to dream a cure.

He got up, clearing his throat. It felt dry. He took a deep breath to cleanse his body. The air around him felt hot. He ran the edge of his hand across his forehead.

His people had always been healthy. Only one plant had been necessary per patient. Now, the sicknesses didn't respond to his medicine. He tried many plants, gathered them, dried them, pounded, seeped, and boiled them. Nothing worked. He needed a new medicine, one strong enough to stop death.

He pulled out his medicine bundle from his pack. He unrolled it, the leather supple. Packets of herbs were bound neatly. In a small bag, he fingered the splinter of wood touched by lightning.

He used it for lancing. His fingers were long; the pads on the fingers were sensitive to the variables of health and sickness in the human body. In his mind's eye, touching a healthy body was like running his fingers across a pond of water so clear you couldn't tell which was air and which was water.

He set aside a bundle of dried salmonberry bark. It was good for the stomach when you ate too much salmon. There were also bundles of dried leaves, stems, and roots of the stinging nettle. He used this for headaches, pain of childbirth, and the ache in the joints of old people. Finally, he found the two packets he'd been looking for: dried strawberry leaves for a tea and twigs from willow to cool a fever.

He made himself tea. He would eat nothing. He would fast and sweat until he was given the new plant for healing. He sipped the tea slowly. He could feel power in this place, but he was beginning to be aware of a strange uneasiness.

He thought of his grandsons. They'd been angry, on edge. His granddaughters had set their jaws firmly, eyes hard and brittle. Their dreams were of fire and strange spotted humans. The medicine man pondered. When had the camp changed? Two moons ago? No, it was when the Ute trader came from the south.

The medicine man had held the wobbling head of an infant as she died. He had smoothed the white hair of an old man who had terrible sores on his body. The man was a cousin. The two had raced together across the meadows when they were young, tiptoed silently beneath the nesting herons, stood watch at the edge of camp. Now, his old friend was dead, along with fourteen others.

He got up and prepared for another sweat.

Inside the lodge, the air was thick. He brewed the willow twigs in the water he'd used to make the steam. He felt the long fronds of willow trees growing down into the darkness, their leaves glowing like bright spears or flashing fish. He felt the heat taking away his flesh, so that his bones became twigs. He was a willow tree bent over rocks and water.

He waited for a vision. He hoped for a plant to save his people. He threw more water on the rocks. The steam rolled off in crushing waves of liquid heat. He felt his chest tighten.

He was the last hope. His knowledge of plants that helped the body was immense, but he needed a deeper vision. He waited, praying.

He didn't feel the ponies gathering in the dark, their hooves heavy and powerful. He didn't see the bears disappearing into their own shadows. He didn't see an old woman beckoning to him.

His hand clutched at his chest. He fell over, head striking the stones, the darkness taking him into itself.

Three nights later, a big storm came up from the west. It blew down the old tree over the silent, cold sweat lodge. The tree fell down on the bones of an old man, bones that became tiny spirit horses, and bones that bears used for dream medicines in their long winter sleep. And bones that flowered from plants gathered by the hands of spirits pure as tears.

Minimal Indian

Now it happened in the twelfth month that James and Crowbar visited Renah, James's sister. They were there to never lift a hand. Just their fork expecting something on it.

The two men drove from Nail, Arkansas, along Highway 16 to Red Star, where Renah had her cabin nearly built into the hills. Her goats and a few hens. A woodpile. Some rusted auto parts Crowbar was thinking of getting for his salvage yard he called *Trucks and Stuff.*

If he could find them under the snow.

And Renah rising early to cook, cooked until after sundown thinking already what to have the next day. Asking for nothing but a trip to the cemetery with a Christmas basket for the parents' graves. If her brother, James, and his friend, Crowbar, had made it across Highway 16 from Nail, they could give her a lift to the graveyard.

What were they doing here, anyway? Expecting their Christmas fruitcake and curls of pork rinds early?

The two men sat at the kitchen table. James stirred his coffee with fury and chopped the eggs on his plate.

Renah cleared her hands.

We open the morning with prayer.

Even before their first bite was swallowed.

EEEEEeeeee. Renah jumped on the curled edge of the linoleum floor when the Spirit moved her. She skitted across the floor in a holy ghost dance. James and Crowbar just looking at her with their mouthful of eggs and toast. Even when she prayed quietly, you could hear James chewing. He might choke, you know, with a mouthful of breakfast. He had to get it down. Crowbar nudged him. But James kept chewing.

You can't hear what she says when you chew, James told him.

It was true. Crowbar tried it.

But Renah kept moving in the Spirit.

And sure enough, soon you could see the drizzling stars dry up. And soon you could see the morning coming from a long way off. Over the curls of cabin smoke. The pine trees and acorns. The morning sun round as an egg basket.

But soon James and Crowbar went back to eating. The truth of the matter was, the ceiling in Arkansas was too high for them. Somewhere up near under heaven, Renah said. They lost interest before they saw too far.

The men lived according to their own ways which were somewhat limited and shortsighted. But they could see the blue sweep of sky across the window.

James, Renah said when she'd prayed.

Whad?

I'd like to take a Christmas basket to the graves.

Id snowed, he said.

I want to go anyway.

Go f' 't, James said.

Renah hummed as she boiled rinse water for the dishes.

James had hoped Crowbar would be a brother-in-law. Renah was not an unhandsome woman, but how could he hand her to Crowbar, Bible-brained as she was? She had black curls kept tight to her head. White skin. A skinny, black-haired, white-skinned woman. One of the strains of back-hill Cherokee. Whose mouth even turned up with the curve of a squirrel tail.

Crowbar owned his business, *Trucks and Stuff,* on the edge of Nail, Arkansas.

He had, after inventory,

two pickups
or what was left of them
a backhoe

a twenty-year-old bus used by a preacher friend of Renah's

a Kenworth cab that parted from its trailer on some back-curve with stubs of grass and dirt still hooked in the door

a rail fence to keep out trespassers
mostly now fallen

a house with a lean-to

an assortment of
crankshafts
fenders
doors
struts
springs
shocks
engine parts

who knew what else

maybe not even Crowbar

the *Trucks and Stuff* sign by the road

a satellite dish
and a fifteen-year-old *James McAdoo for Sheriff* sign in his yard.

Politics was still the latest.

Bigger than satellite dishes.

Crowbar would be a good husband for Renah.

James didn't know why Renah never married. Maybe no one asked her. No. That wasn't true. There was Sam Jackson from *Sam's Bait and Tackle* over on Bull Shoals who had asked her.

And there was the traveling tool salesman.

Family meant something to Renah. She had their photos lined up on the kitchen walls and along the top of the pie-safes and on lace doilies that their grandmother had tatted. Hairpin lace or something like that. The old women always had their hands going. Back and forth like a litter of birds in the trees. All chirped up all the time.

A regular backhoe at anyone who passed. Dredging up.

Renah could do it. You got the whole story from her. Whether you wanted it or not.

The only thing she cut off, when she was behind the camera, was the heads in the photos, or at least above the nose so you kind of had to guess who it was by their trousers or dress.

She was a good woman, though.

After breakfast, Renah fed the hens and goats, and James and

Crowbar drove Renah to the cemetery in the snow.

Renah had her Brownie camera with her.

She decided she wouldn't get out of the car, but honked James and Crowbar in the direction they should go with the Christmas basket for the parents. Since James couldn't remember. Or couldn't find the graves under the cover of snow.

Over this way.

Honk.

Now that.

Honk.

Not that way.

Honk.

Renah motioned them one way then another. Back to the left. There, James.

Honk.

In the car, Renah was warm as if she'd never left her cast-iron bed in the kitchen all heaped with her string-tied rag quilts in the darkest purples and browns and maroons.

James and Crowbar swept snow from the graves.

Renah took a photo of James and Crowbar placing the basket.

I wasn't even turned around, Crowbar said.

Won'd make no difference, James answered. There'd be nothin' of us from the ears up in her picture, anyway.

The car radio played Christmas music as they drove back to the road.

Then an advertisement for Burleens' hair salon.

An Evangelist saying hallelujah to the snow-covered morning.

And the Singing Starbrites!

Those sisters:

Juanita
Bonita
Corita
Danita.

Their mother spit 'em out like peas.

James waved to a car that passed. Another Cherokee. A marginal Indian to the ones powwowing and migrating and buffaloing on the plains.

The Cherokee had been a robed and turbaned tribe with curled-handled pipes, writing and reading the letters of Sequoyah's syllabary.

Full of superstitions and little-people tales, unless they'd been converted to Christianity. Even at that, they were still full of both worlds. Sometimes conjuring. Sometimes singing hymns. Not knowing anything about being an Indian.

But a somewhat farming
backyard-hung-with-quilts
canning-jar-cellared-for-a-long-winter
vegetable-patched-in-summer
few-hogged
sort of folk.

Dry goods on the shelf
a bag of material scraps in the corner

egg baskets
apple baskets
one- and two-pie baskets
berry baskets
potato baskets
market baskets

froes
mallets
drawknives
string
strips of oak and willow for more baskets

bittersweet
sage
herbs hanging by the woodstove

What kind of Indian that?

Their backwoods jamming was enough to keep a regular Indian
out.

James and Crowbar hadn't been converted, Renah knew. She
remembered them climbing out the vestibule window of the New
Covenant Church.

That's why they'd come to Red Star from Nail! The Spirit had
delivered them to Renah for another chance to be saved. Hallelujah. She tossed in the seat as they drove back toward her cabin.
Especially when they came over the hills, and saw into the distance of Arkansas.

They still almost could see the smoke from the old Cherokee
pipes in the winter fog rising off the ice in the streams and farm
ponds.

She told James and Crowbar how the ancestors had walked from the southeast on a forced march. Most kept going to Oklahoma. But theirs stopped here.

Except for the hand of God they wouldn't have made it.

It was a haunted land. A magical kingdom of animal transformations and mutations of borders. Too much knowledge of the old ways. When no one would talk about it. That's what they did. And a Christian God to whom they had to make a commitment. Who could come for them anytime.

There could be a revolution in Arkansas from the suppression of the old ways. Anytime. Gunshot heard nightly. Everyone digging in. Like squirrels spread-legged in the yard. Trying to uncover.

The Cherokee seemed like everyone else. Maybe another language leaping out once in a while. Little people under the house. Chimney smoke dancing on its front legs over the yard. Its hind legs in the air. But God waited for their decision. Just like everybody else.

I can see up into heaven, Renah said. Just up to God's ears. I can see his son, Jesus, standing by his throne, a halo bright as an egg yoke hanging over his head. A book on how to *save the lost* under his hand. I can see God's old truck parked behind his throne. I can see the long white hair that hangs to his shoulders. I just can't see his face.

James looked at Crowbar.

We'd be BLIND if we did. Renah's voice was rising again like heat from the woodstove, if they'd been in her kitchen instead of James's car. We can't stand the sight of purity. Here on earth. In these plank-floored cabins and leaning fields. The low roofs and high floors.

Yo, James said. It feels sometimes like my head is goint to meet my knees when I'm sitting at your table.

The roof leaks snow, Renah told James. If it warms up, I'll have to get the buckets, James. Otherwise I see it coming through like the joy of heaven.

Yes.

The former and latter rain often fell all day in buckets on Renah's floor. Maybe James and Crowbar could repair the leaks.

Maybe Renah could marry, and her husband could fix it.

James ate an apple from the basket as they listened to Renah.

Got another one? Crowbar asked.

The men chewed.

An apple works just like a piece of toast, James said.

It was another day under God's grace. He must be in his hip boots and fishing gear. Warming his truck in his garage. Yes, God had it wrapped up. Had his inventory in line. His family photographs on the wall. His angels with their bright wings. Renah could almost see their faces, though she could hear their wings beating like a fan belt.

EEEEEeeee.

How those Starbrites could sing:

Juanita
Bonita
Corita
Dorita.

Wuuh. Whhuuu. James and Crowbar could see their voices up there on the stage.

Around a curve in Newton County, just east of the Boston Mountains, a farmer's truck loaded with chickens crossed the center line and hit James and Crowbar and Renah head-on.

There were chicken feathers and splintered chicken crates everywhere.

Renah stood up and shook herself off. Well, she was light as a feather herself. She walked down the road. Where was she going? What happened?

She saw James and Crowbar dazed in the truck.

Hens were flying up to heaven on their little wings like snow. Renah didn't know they could fly. Up over Arkansas. Past the wood-carvers in their cabins. Past hog farmers and turkey barns. The rocky soil. Logging trucks. Her goats and hens. She even saw the steam from the Dardanelle Nuclear Power Plant on Interstate 40. The dam that Renah spelled d.a.m.b. whenever she said it. That's the way you heard it around her. She wouldn't have it any other way.

And there was some sort of funny tag on her ear.

Renah even saw heaven spread out before her like hills in the distance of Arkansas. The trees were the heads of everyone who had called the name of Jesus.

And now she could see GOD.

She could see HE looked a little like Floyd Buber, her father's old friend.

She turned to tell James and Crowbar.

But they had their heads caught in the fork of a tree. And the Spirit of the air wouldn't let them pass.

They suddenly looked monkey-faced, and disappeared. Renah cried out, and tried to rush after them, but she heard the angels singing.

She saw the very face of GOD. Not just ears and nose as she imaged she'd seen his body on the throne. But a whole forehead full of stars. A nose with two garages. A mouth like the opening of a backwood cave. Some sort of engineering design on his face. Well, he was a regular computer chip. She'd seen a magazine in a doctor's office once. A complicated crossroads of veins and connectives. A numbered face full of more than she could recognize at first. A whole being full of life and love.

The Starbrites had been right.

The bait date she ended with Sam Jackson when she told him of her love for GOD, and he took off the next day back to Bull Shoals.

The traveling tool salesman likewise.

But this God. And there was his son. He was the one who waited for her. He was in his old jeans down there at the end of the road where she now walked. Just like her vision had seen.

What You Have

A crucifix on a bare wall. Crocheted cincture
with a lover's knot tied at each end, which swing
as you walk (also known as "nun's balls"). The veil, with
or without wimple. Crepe-soled, lace-up oxfords, black,
or sandals, preferably Dr. Scholl's. A watch,
plain, and your pectoral cross on a black string—
small enamel for annual vows, ebony for
perpetual. Your breviary with homemade
cover from fabric out of common stock. Grosgrain
bookmarks: anchor, heart, and cross. Your prayer list, tidy
and alphabetical when young, fragmented, much
amended when old (having been at it so long).
Underwear: invariably white cotton, though
colors have been seen among the postulants. Night-
gowns ornate, though some sleep nude in the sight of God.
A plain gold wedding ring—your mother's or your own.
A plot of earth by the chapel near the apple
orchard. Your constant mind. Your viscera. Your bones.

Habit

It descends with the Holy Spirit over
your face, breasts, legs, draping
the flesh in modesty, a falling curtain
of grace, and you: an empty dress-shape
with a scapular, a cincture, and a veil,
receptacle of God's will.
      Unless, of course, your body
is a swamp of desire, your heart
a simmering kettle, its shriek
clamped behind the grinding
and the grinding of your teeth.
Then your habit is a white enameled stove,
and you a roasting crackling pig inside,
on whom time will work the inevitable:
an implosion of self-immolation, or the blast outside.
And you: a projectile trailing the shreds of habit,
flames of rage and hunger your
contrail into the world.

On Going In

O Lord my God, in thee do I put my trust.
Save me from them that pursue me and deliver me,
Lest they tear my soul like a lion.

I.

The torment of voices:
When are you going
to get...
When are you going
to be...
Who will you pick who will
pick you
like a fruit coming into
juice waiting to squirt
and burst
at the first squeeze?
And the boys: their busy faces.
And the urgency of men and their
verbs: screw, suck, bang,
squeeze.
And the infinitive future: to bear,
to wash, to feed, to do—and do,
and do. How do the other girls
see Romance
where I see the alien hair
curling over waistbands
barely contained?
What is it doing there?
The things underneath are after me:
they want in,
they want to go in,
and once in, they will never—
like a fish hook with a barb—
come out again.
Yet by this passionate device

it is intended
that I sacrifice
my life.

II.

And must it be beneath
a veil of white, a bride
like Iphigenia—all aflutter—
not understanding
the nature of the knife?
Something will go in, poor girl.
It hardly matters if it's steel
or the recondite flesh
or which man it is
with a thing in his hand
which he points at your chest
and then—at the last second—
deflects beneath
the shrouds of your hem.
Your destiny is written in
the stars: you are
a lamb. You are
delicious. You are
a sacrifice.

III.

The essence of escape
is in concealment. Yes,
my veil is white. Yes,
yes, I will vow a vow
for life, and none will doubt
the fullness of my
sacrifice. My man is
big; the biggest man
there is. And the stars
sing with delight

at my destiny—
I'm getting married—
to the ideal man.
He has no thing.
He wants no thing
from me. His verbs are
love and sacrifice
but his nouns
are remote as the heavens,
the sound of beating wings—
Oh, God!
I got away!
And all that is expected
of this bride
is that she pray.

THYLIAS MOSS

Mornings

To every morning reach
for the wire whisk, the yellow bag
of sugar above her head
on the top shelf next to dried beans.
And the eggs of Rhode Island Reds
that maybe were how she felt
mornings
before putting on her face.
She was someone else making pancakes
blank and plain
who could crack eggs, who did;
who could break a ruler over knuckles
given the chance, given a face.
Every morning to do this.

The pancakes were round
and unlike moons, rounder, necessary,
perfect, stacked only four or five high,
the repressed architecture of the kitchen.

She cut doors into her stack and
the forked and knifed windows weakened
the structure good then only for syrup.
The napkin across her lap lay there
the most obedient thing in the house.

The scene changes as it must for this
to be a story, not a moment out of context.
There was more to it than mornings, more
than the initial wondering and fussing

over clouds or sun; the rain could fall
in many tempos, summon all of the violence
available to clear drops of water and fail
to wean anyone. It is idle in the barrels
and in the night-stand glass she reaches for
in darkness first, then him.

In her secret place, deep there, the place
in her mind she can't find her way back to
is a face she blocks with her hand these mornings
reaching for a box of pancake mix
that she empties into a painted Pyrex bowl
and stirs, flour on her fingertips as before
though not the same, the face on the box smiles
and takes the credit which so far this morning
is just weather

such as there was long ago
when apple blossoms might be cotton
and the flowers dark girls wore in their
rough cotton hair cotton too.
Pick me, take me to the fair.
There are blue streaks
in Auntie's hair, from the blue rinse Doreen,
Auntie's beautician, recommends, Doreen
whose lifeline is blue now and unpredictable.
Says Doreen: *Kindness makes up for fairness.*

There must be some pleasure in this
for life is not complete without it
and her life is almost over; there just
isn't any room for more living; death
is most practical that way and decomposition
that makes mix of all willing.
      When she succeeds
in putting on her face, the eye liner, the

foundation, the shadow, she will smile
like the woman on the box, but not at her;
she smiles at the suffering Savior
and while doing so can't get *crucify him*
through her teeth.

Lot's Wife

after Akhmatova

They had no time—the just man
hurried across the bridge,
followed God's magistrate
along the black ridge.

His grieving wife lagged behind
as if she had no will,
arms heavy with useless things,
heart heavier still.

She couldn't recall if she'd shut the door,
turned off the iron; worse guilt,
she'd left behind the baby pictures,
her mother's ring, her wedding quilt.

One arm raised as if to gather
her whole life in that embrace,
tears blurring the view,
without much thought she turned her face,

became what she had shed. Who grieves
for this nameless woman, Lot's reflective wife?
I grieve.
I know holding on can cost a life.

Milk

How many nurses cared for her needs? The first dressed Bea's wound, a puckered red mouth silenced with staples. A second nurse brought her a cup of chilled juice to wash away the sour taste in her mouth. A third nurse, a man, massaged her sore back.

Then a fourth nurse came in, a small, dark-haired woman with a pen in her curls. She knelt beside Bea's bed and covered her feet with blue paper slippers, then helped Bea to stand and shuffle to the bathroom. Her bladder was bursting, but everything below her waist was so numb that nothing came out. When she finally gave up, the toilet bowl was gory with blood and clots of tissue. Had a mess like this really come from her body? Even as she stood there, blood dripped to the floor. She bent to wipe it up and near-ly passed out. Too embarrassed to ask the nurse to do this for her, she left the blood on the tiles. The nurse handed her a belt and a sanitary napkin as thick as a book, then helped Bea lie down.

"If you need anything at all pull that cord by your bed and ask for Patrice." The nurse tapped a pill into Bea's palm. "Do you want your baby?" she said.

She was asking, of course, if Bea wanted to see him. But the question Bea heard was: Do you want to keep the baby you've just given birth to?

She hadn't conceived him on purpose—she had slept with a man without taking precautions, like an ignorant schoolgirl. But she had decided to keep him. She had worked with abstractions for so many years she had forgotten it was possible to sometimes catch a glimpse of the thing in itself. When she realized that a fetus was growing in the universe deep in her womb, she couldn't bear to abort it. She talked to it for months, asking it questions. She looked forward to meeting it as she would have looked for-ward to meeting an alien who could tell her what life on another planet was like. But for now she was tired. She swallowed the pill, then slept like a woman who's been up for three days and has just given birth to an eleven-pound child.

She awoke to a gong. Cheering. Applause. A floor-length blue curtain surrounded her bed. From beyond it came the sounds of a television set turned up full volume.

An orderly brought soup. The warm, salty broth tasted so delicious Bea savored each sip. Then she turned to watch the sun set above the river; the buildings dissolved until only the lights in their windows were visible. A distant observer would have guessed that the city was nothing more substantial than a few panes of glass with light bulbs behind them, as earthly astronomers had assumed for so long that the universe was made of comets and stars, of things they could see. Instead, it turned out that all but a fraction of the cosmos was dark invisible matter—black holes? some new gas? giant cold planets?

She looked around, as if someone could see her thinking about invisible matter instead of her child. She heard her roommate say: *Lie still, stop your wiggling.* Bea was certain that if she could watch another mother diaper her baby she would learn to do this herself, but the heavy blue curtain blocked the woman from view.

Bea didn't see her roommate until late that afternoon, though the woman's TV was on the whole time—soap operas, game shows, even cartoons. Every so often the woman groaned: *Huh, huh, huh.* Then, about four, the curtain rings squealed and Bea's roommate emerged. She was short, but so broad that her johnny wouldn't close, exposing a black swatch of buttocks and spine. She was thirty, maybe older, her hair short and shapeless. Crooked in one arm was a half-naked child; in the other hand, a diaper. She scuffed to the bathroom in her blue paper slippers without glancing at Bea. After ten or fifteen minutes she opened the door and scuffed beyond the curtain.

When Bea hobbled to the bathroom to use the toilet herself, she saw a mustardy smear on the lid of the trash can. Why hadn't the woman wiped up her baby's feces? *Because blacks aren't clean.* This thought upset her, of course. Wasn't it more logical that her roommate simply hadn't noticed the dirt? Or she still was too weak to juggle a baby and a wet paper towel? She probably had left the smear where it was in the confidence that the janitor would wipe it away. The next time he came, though, he left the smear on the can, and the stain of Bea's blood on the tiles near the bowl.

The nurse rolled a Plexiglas crib through the curtain. The baby inside was swaddled in blankets. His eyes were screwed tight but his mouth was wide open, like the mouth of a pitcher waiting for someone to fill it with milk.

"He's hungry," Patrice said. She lay the child in Bea's lap, across her incision.

This is my son, Bea said to herself, over and over, but the fact seemed unreal. He was fair, she was dark. He was heavy and round, with a triple chin and jowls, she was gaunt, with high cheekbones. (Did he look like his father? She could barely recall.)

"What's his name?" Patrice asked.

"Isaac," Bea told her, and, as she named him, he suddenly seemed real.

"Isaac," Patrice repeated. "Biblical names are so full of meaning."

Bea didn't bother to explain that she had named her son after Sir Isaac Newton.

"Time to get started," Patrice said. "Your milk won't come in until tomorrow at least, but you both need the practice."

Bea weighed a breast in one palm: a Baggie with a spoonful of milk in the bottom. She lifted her son. He was crying from hunger but wouldn't turn his head to suck.

"Here's the trick," Patrice said. Gripping Bea's nipple, she rubbed it across the baby's damp cheek.

As if by arrangement, Isaac turned toward the nipple and opened his mouth. When he clamped down his gums, the pain was so intense that Bea cried out and jerked back. He was wailing more shrilly. She let him latch on again, steeling herself not to push him away. The pain slowly abated. Still, as he sucked, she felt a vague irritation, as if a street corner beggar kept pulling at her arm.

"That's enough," Patrice said, just as Bea started to feel more at ease. "I'll take him to the nursery. Here's a pamphlet to study." On the cover was a mother in a lacy white nightgown smiling down at an infant nuzzling her breast. "A bruiser like this will want to eat every hour. He'll be an eating machine. You've got to relax!"

It was after eleven but Bea couldn't sleep. In another few days she would have to take her child home. She had never been alone with a baby. Her mother lived in Cleveland and was legally blind. Few of her friends or colleagues had children. She'd read books about babies, but she sensed that a new kind of knowledge was called for.

Still, she might sleep if only her roommate would turn off her TV. Bea hated to ask, but if she did so politely, pleading the strains of their common ordeal... She crossed the room, barefoot, and nudged the curtain aside.

The woman sat with her knees drawn to her chest, her baby propped against her shins. She was watching a talk show whose dapper black host Bea knew she should recognize. He said something about a basketball player named Larry and the woman snorted through her nose.

"I didn't mean to disturb you. It's just, well, it's late."

The woman seemed to expect that Bea would do what she had to—take her pulse or draw blood—and leave her alone. She stared at the screen with such a fierce gravity that nothing leaked out; she seemed to have imploded in on herself like a light-eating star.

"Your baby," Bea said, just to make herself known. But then, to determine what to say next, she had to look at the child. It wore a frilly pink dress. Thick auburn hair curled past its ears and its coppery-brown skin was lustrous and smooth. "She's...pretty," Bea said.

"Huh. That child ain't no she." The woman said this without moving her lips.

Bea shut her eyes to concentrate. "Oh, I'm sorry. I didn't—"

"Ain't your fault. Didn't I buy all these dresses? How's anyone supposed to know a baby's a boy if he's wearing a dress?"

The thought crossed Bea's mind that only a poor, uneducated woman would predict her baby's sex based on old wives' tales. "You thought you'd have a girl?"

" 'Thought' nothing. Those doctors took a picture with that

sound thing, said they couldn't see no johnson, I had me a girl."

Bea felt suddenly ashamed, as she did when a colleague found a mistake in a paper she'd written. The baby started to fuss. Though his mother's huge breasts swelled beneath her johnny and were ringed with wet cloth, she poked a bottle in his mouth. Bea almost believed the woman had done this to spite her. "What's his name?" she asked, to justify the length of time she'd stood staring.

"Only name he's got is fit for a girl. Can't think of no new name until I ask his father. Man don't like it, his boy gets some name he ain't said he liked."

Bea couldn't help but think that a man who cared so much about his son's name ought to have been able to attend the boy's birth. "Did you have a Caesarean?" She asked this for reasons she didn't like to admit: if the woman said no, she might leave the next day and be replaced by a roommate who wouldn't make Bea self-conscious or watch TV all the time. "Or was it natural?" she said, to mask her suspicion that the woman didn't know what "Caesarean" meant.

" 'Natural,' huh. Last time I was in here I had me twin girls. Doctors cut my belly open, I went home in two days. This time I had this teensy little boy, came out on his own the minute I got here, no cutting, no drugs, I can barely stand up. Hurts me down there like a sonofabitch."

The woman pushed the buttons on her remote until she found the news. A snowstorm. A plane crash. The mayor of Washington had just been arrested for buying cocaine. According to his lawyer, the mayor had been framed by government officials waging a vendetta against powerful blacks.

"Huh!" She faced Bea. "What you think? Think he's guilty?"

Did she? Of course. "He's innocent until they prove he isn't," Bea said.

Whatever the test she'd been given, she'd failed. The woman rolled toward the curtain, her backside toward Bea and her fleshy black forearm shielding her son. Then she seemed to fall asleep as a movie about the attack on Pearl Harbor unrolled its credits over Bea's head.

·　　·　　·

Someone was jiggling Bea's leg.

"I'm sorry," Patrice said, "but you'll have to get used to it." Patrice handed her Isaac. He was crying again. "I don't want to worry you, but if you can't feed him soon we'll have to give him formula. Then he won't want to suck. And if that happens, well, your milk will never come in."

His mouth worked her nipple. Where was this milk supposed to come from? she wondered. Why couldn't she simply will it to be?

The baby sucked at each side for exactly eight minutes; Patrice timed him, eyes trained on her sharply cocked wrist.

"You don't have to do that," Bea said. She heard an unfamiliar edge in her voice.

The nurse stopped and stood blinking. She picked at the beads trimming her sweater as if these were burrs. It occurred to Bea then that Patrice was as uncomfortable with people as she was. Unlike the other nurses Patrice couldn't seem to sense what a patient might want. Bea pitied her for being so poorly suited to the job she had chosen, as she pitied the student who had been her advisee for the past seven years; he thought that *having vision* meant seeing stars clearly through the lens of a telescope.

Patrice stopped picking at her sweater. "Never mind," she said. "I can be that way sometimes. We'll try again tomorrow." She wheeled the crib toward the door. Beyond the blue curtain she said to Bea's roommate: "Wake up there! Wake up! Just think, you could crush her! Here, let me take her back to the nursery."

"Uh-uh. You leave that baby right where he is. I don't want my baby in no nursery."

Bea wondered if her roommate really believed that the nurses would purposely try to harm her son. She was being… what was it? Paranoid, Bea thought. Then she drifted to sleep.

It was just after breakfast. A girl with red hair poked her face through the curtain. "Statistics," she said. She consulted her clipboard. "Are you Beatrice Weller?"

Bea nodded.

"Maiden name?"

"Beatrice Weller."

The girl regarded Bea closely. She asked what Bea "did."

"I'm a cosmologist," Bea said. She started to explain that cosmologists were scientists who studied the universe—how it formed, how it grew. But the girl interrupted.

"You do makeup? And hair?"

Bea surprised herself by saying "Um. Sure. Um-hm."

"Do you mind if I ask how much you charge for making someone over? Before, you know? And after? Could you maybe do me?"

"Oh, no," Bea said. "I couldn't. I don't have my...tools."

The girl seemed disappointed. "Are you sure? It's important. I mean, there's this guy I just met...You'll think I'm silly...but maybe, I don't know, you could give me some tips? I get paid Wednesday morning." She leaned forward, head cocked, her palms pressed together.

"Well. I suppose. I'll be here until Friday." She would think of something later. Already she sensed that, once you began, it was easy to say things you didn't mean.

"Oh, thanks!" the girl said. She asked a few last questions: Bea's nationality (U.S.) and her age (thirty-six). "I'm sure you had the sense not to smoke or use drugs while you were pregnant." She made a mark on a form, promised to return for her beauty consultation, then dragged a chair behind the curtain. "Hello? Coreen Jones?"

Since the name was so common it had the effect of making Bea's roommate seem less real, not more so, as if she weren't a person but a whole class of objects: *chair, atom, Jones.*

Bea couldn't help but eavesdrop. Coreen mumbled her answers, which the girl asked her to repeat again and again, her voice louder each time.

"You're unemployed?"

"No, I ain't."

"You've got a job?" the girl asked. "Where?"

"At a school."

"You've got a job at a school?"

"Don't worry," Coreen mumbled. "All I do is cook there."

And so on, until the girl asked Coreen for the name of her child.

"Ain't got one."

"Excuse me?"

"I said my baby doesn't have no name."

"She doesn't have a name?"

"It's a he, not a she, and he doesn't have a name."

Tell her, Bea thought. *It isn't your fault. You're not a bad mother.* But Coreen explained nothing.

The girl asked Coreen if her child had a father.

"Think I done it myself?"

"I *meant* are you married."

"Man never needed no piece of paper to make him a father."

The girl asked for his name. Coreen mumbled an answer. "Can you spell that?" the girl asked.

"Always make sure I can spell a man's name before I have his baby." Coreen spelled the letters slowly: "N–A–T–E..." This ordeal over, the girl asked Coreen for her "ethnic category."

"American," Coreen said.

"Oh, no," said the girl, "I mean, where were you born?"

"America," Coreen said.

"Well, what country do you *come* from?"

"Come from? Way back? Guess you could say Sierra Leone."

"That's not a country. It's a mountain. In Mexico."

"Sure it's a country. Sierra Leone."

"All right, then, where is it?"

"West Africa," Coreen said.

"But that's not a country! You mean *South* Africa."

Bea heard Coreen grunt. "Huh, you so smart, you put down whatever country you want. You got any more questions?"

"Only one," the girl said. "Now, try to think hard. Did you use alcohol, or smoke cigarettes, or take any drugs at all—heroin, or cocaine, or even marijuana—while your child was inside you?"

A pause. Bea was startled to hear Coreen laugh.

"Girl, if I done all that awful shit to my baby, he wouldn't have turned out so *perfect,* now would he."

Bea had just spent another fruitless half-hour nursing her son when a woman's harsh voice barked over the intercom that the photographer was there to take pictures of their babies, but they had to line up by the door to Room 3 within the next fifteen minutes or forfeit their chance. She usually considered taking pictures to be vulgar and vain. But if something were to happen to Isaac, she thought, she wouldn't have a picture to remember what he looked like.

From behind the blue curtain came the sounds of her roommate preparing her child. Bea took Isaac as he was, in a hospital T-shirt stamped BETH ZION, BETH ZION, as if this were his name. The two women wheeled their babies' cribs down the hall. Every few steps Coreen clutched her belly. Her forehead was wet, her face ashen.

"Are you all right?" Bea asked. "If you want, I could take him—" She was suddenly afraid Coreen would react with the same paranoia she had shown toward Patrice.

Coreen mumbled what sounded like "tell me I'm fine" and kept pushing the crib.

They lined up behind a dozen other women. The black mothers seemed half Coreen's age, their hair pulled up high, all beads and stiff braids. Their babies, like hers, were dressed in fancy outfits; one of the boys wore suspenders and a bow tie. A middle-aged woman in a pink linen suit handed out brochures. Bea saw the cheapest price and nearly turned back. But when would Isaac be a newborn again? She wiped the spittle from his mouth. He gnawed at her finger with sharply ridged gums.

"Huh!" Coreen said. "How come they never tell you what things like this cost till you're standing in line?"

Bea expected her roommate to wheel her baby's crib back to their room. How could she afford twenty dollars for a picture? Bad enough she was spending an extra five dollars a day for TV, an expense Bea herself, from years of living on a stipend, had elected to save.

But Coreen stayed in line. She filled out the form, holding it against the back of the Puerto Rican woman standing in front of her. She let the photographer perch her son on a pillow and snap a light in his face.

"I'm not buying it right now," she told the woman in pink. "But you better take good care of it. That boy's bound to be famous. Reporters need his picture, you just might be *rich*."

Bea hadn't wanted anyone to see her until she'd gotten the hang of taking care of her baby. She'd disconnected the phone, but in the middle of the week a boy in a Mohawk brought her a towering basket of fruit. "Congratulations on your own Little Bang!" read the card. "From the crew." Her friend Modhumita, who worked in a lab not far from the hospital, stopped by every day. Bea caught herself hoping that her roommate would see Mita's dusky brown skin and think she was black.

Coreen's phone rang often, but no one came to visit. From what Bea could tell, none of Coreen's friends could get time off from work, or they couldn't leave their children. As the TV set blared, Coreen told a friend what she hadn't told Bea.

Her "pains" had begun on the subway to work. "Know what scared is?" she said. "Scared's thinking you're gonna drop your baby right there on that nasty old floor, all those white boys looking up your nookie."

Instead of getting off at the stop near the school, Coreen had taken the train to her clinic downtown. "Time I get inside I can't hardly walk, they say I'm still closed, I got a month to go, it's only false pains. I say, 'You ain't careful, you gonna have yourself a false little baby right there in your lap,' but they don't want to hear it. I go out and call Lena and ask could she keep the twins a while longer. Then I call me an ambulance. Time it pulls up, driver says, 'How come you people always waiting till the last minute? You like giving birth to your babies outdoors?'"

Her friend must have asked a question.

"Nate?" Coreen said. "He's away on some haul, don't even know yet." She complained she didn't feel well, she was all hot and cold and she hurt something awful. Then she shushed whoever was on the other end of the phone because the announcer was saying that the police had a videotape of Marion Barry smoking cocaine in that Washington hotel room, and not with his wife.

"Huh!" Coreen said. "They got that nigger by the balls. Let him try to lie now!"

After dinner that night Patrice brought in Isaac. He worked Bea's nipples so hard he raised a welt on his lip, but still no milk came.

"He's losing weight," Patrice told her. "You'll have to calm down. Just look at his face and think loving thoughts."

But the baby kept crying. His face was red as lava; his mouth might have been a crater into which she'd been ordered to leap. According to Patrice, if her milk didn't come in within twenty-four hours they would have to give him formula.

"Hey!" Coreen called. "I need me a doctor."

Patrice shot Bea a glance, then flung the curtain aside. "You're just engorged," she said. "That means your breasts are too full. We'll have to dry you up. Then you'll feel better."

Bea wondered why her roommate wasn't nursing her child. Didn't she know it was healthier and cheaper to breast-feed? Maybe she disliked the feel of a mouth tugging at her nipple as much as Bea herself did. Or perhaps she couldn't afford to stay home with the baby. Bea stared at the curtain. Why could she imagine what was going on a thousand light-years away, but not beyond that drape?

In the middle of the night she heard Coreen moaning, "Help me. Lord, help me. I'm freezing. Lord help me."

Bea stood from bed, wobbling, and pushed the curtain aside. Coreen lay with her head thrown back on her pillow, her johnny pulled low as if she'd clawed at the neck. Her breasts were exposed, dark, hard, and full, rippling with veins; they looked like two hemispheres carved from mahogany, the North and South Poles rising from each.

"I'm freezing. I'm dying." She was shaking so violently that the bed squeaked beneath her. Her blanket lay on the floor.

Slowly Bea bent, gathered Coreen's blanket, then lifted herself by the rail on the bed. She drew the cotton cloth over her roommate. Her wrist brushed Coreen's arm. Bea flinched away, scorched.

She pulled the cord for the nurse, then tugged the blanket from her own bed and spread it over Coreen. The shaking didn't stop.

Patrice came. "What's the matter? Tell me what's wrong."

"She's freezing," Bea told her. "She said she feels like she's dying."

Patrice took Bea's arm and led her back through the drape. "She's just being melodramatic," Patrice whispered. "The state gives them formula. They can't bear to turn down something for free. I'll get her an ice pack. She'll be fine, don't you worry."

Bea glanced at the curtain. "I'll get a doctor myself."

Patrice stalked from the room. Bea pushed through the drape. She didn't know what to do, so she stood there and waited. Without the window, this side of the room was so gloomy that she almost reached up to switch on the TV.

"Don't."

Her heart jumped.

"Don't let them take him." It seemed to cost Coreen a great deal to speak. "Don't," she repeated.

"I promise," Bea said. But already Coreen had started thrashing again and she didn't seem to hear.

The baby was sleeping face-down in his crib. When Bea lifted him, he hung limp from her hands, surprisingly light compared to her own child. She carried him the way one might carry a puppy, then sat on her bed. He lay so still. Was he breathing? She stroked his curls, then his neck. He turned toward her belly, his cheek nestling her thigh. He moved his lips. Her breasts tingled.

A doctor came. Bea huddled closer to the child, partly for warmth and partly to hide him, from what she didn't know. What would she do if someone tried to take him?

The doctor asked Coreen this or that question; he called her "Miss Jones" and murmured "I see" after each of her answers. Then he slowly explained that she had an infection called en-do-me-tri-tis. "It's really quite rare for a natural birth, but sometimes it happens." He sounded offhand, though Bea knew this was something that women used to die from before antibiotics. "We'll put in an IV—that's an intravenous line—and you'll feel better before long."

The baby stirred in Bea's lap. He looked up but didn't cry, as if he understood it was in his best interest to lie very still. His smooth copper skin reminded Bea of the telescope her father had bought her the day she turned twelve. She had held it for hours, until the sun set, certain it would bring her the power to *see*. The child in her lap seemed to hold this same promise. Unlike her own son, he appeared to want nothing.

A sweet-faced young woman—Korean? Japanese?—wheeled an

IV pole next to Bea's bed. She must have been a medical student, Bea thought; she had the overly serious expression of someone who is hiding how uncertain she feels.

"Here," the student said, "let me take... Is that your baby?"

Bea held the boy closer, hiding his face. "You want my roommate, Coreen Jones."

"Oh," the student said. She still seemed confused, but wheeled the pole through the curtain. "Hello," she said. "Don't worry, I'll be done in a minute. It won't hurt one bit."

Bea could hear her roommate mutter, "You ain't got it in."

"Just a minute... right there..."

"Missed by a mile, girl. Might as well've stuck that thing in my ear." Coreen mumbled these words; if Bea hadn't grown accustomed to hearing Coreen's voice, she wouldn't have known what she'd said. It was almost as if Coreen had been trying for so many years not to be understood that she no longer knew how to say what she meant.

The student kept up her patter—"See, that didn't hurt"—and Coreen stopped complaining. When Bea carried the baby back to his crib, his mother lay snoring, the blanket Bea had given her pulled to her chin.

The statistician returned. "I got paid!" She waved a check. "We've got twenty-four hours to create a new me."

Bea was changing Isaac's diaper, holding his ankles in the air with one hand and swabbing yellow stool from his bottom with the other. She hadn't washed her hair since she'd come to the hospital. She wore tortoiseshell glasses she'd picked out in ninth grade. "I'm really very tired—"

"Just one little tip?"

Bea stared at the girl. What was the name of that stuff on her eyes? Liner? Mascara? "Maybe you could use less... shadow," she said. As she taped Isaac's diaper and wiped his feces from her hands, she searched for a phrase from the glamour magazines her mother used to buy her. "Let the real you come through."

"The real me?" She seemed baffled. "Well, my friends always say I'm a typical redhead."

Bea could hear Coreen groan. "I meant your *best* self," she said.

"Let your best self shine through."

"But how?" the girl asked.

Bea shrugged. *Read a book. Try to imagine how a child comes to be.* "That's the same advice I give to all my clients."

The girl nodded gravely. "I'll try it," she said. She again waved the check. "How much do I owe you?"

Bea flapped her hand, a gesture that made her feel both generous and mean.

"Thanks!" the girl said. "I'll let you know how it goes." On her way to the hall she stopped to chat with Coreen. "How *are* you?" she asked. "I just wanted to tell you . . . I looked in an atlas, and Sierra Leone was right there in West Africa, just like you said!"

Coreen got a visit from a tired-sounding woman who seemed to run the clinic where Coreen had received her prenatal care.

"What's this?" the doctor said. "Who put in this IV?" She summoned Patrice. "Just look at this arm, the way it's all blown up. My patient's IV has been draining into everything *but* her vein— for how long? Ten, fifteen hours? Where do you think all that fluid's been going?"

The doctor couldn't stay—another of her patients was about to deliver—but she gave Patrice instructions as to what to do next.

"I didn't put this in," Patrice grumbled when the doctor had gone. "I would never do a job as sloppy as this."

"Huh," Coreen said. "If I treated hamburger meat as sloppy as you treat the folks in these beds, they would fire my ass."

Coreen was feeling better, but her baby was sick. "He shits all the time," she told the pediatrician.

"Oh, all newborn babies have frequent movements," he said. He sounded like the same well-meaning young man who'd given Isaac his checkup. (*The nurse tells me that you and your baby aren't bonding,* he'd said. *Is there anything I can do?*, as shy as a boy whose mother has asked him to unhook her brassiere.)

"Ain't just frequent," Coreen told him. "And the color ain't right."

He started to say that all newborn babies had odd-colored "movements."

"Don't you think I know what a baby's shit looks like? Didn't I raise myself twins?"

His voice tensed. "I'll look into it. But I'm sure if the nurses had seen anything amiss, I would have been notified."

Bea assumed he was right, until she remembered that, even at her sickest, Coreen had changed her baby's diapers herself.

Coreen's boyfriend came to visit. Bea saw nothing but his running shoes, caked with dry mud, as they moved back and forth beneath the blue curtain. She could hear when he kissed his son, then Coreen.

"Go on," Coreen said. "I'm too sore for that stuff."

Bea wondered if Coreen lived with this man. Would he come to take her home? Would he help her care for their son?

The boyfriend, it seemed, drove a moving van or truck. He'd been on a trip to some city out west. How could he have know that Coreen would give birth to their child five weeks early? When no one answered at home he called the hospital from a pay phone, but someone at the switchboard kept cutting him off. He drove without stopping until he'd reached Boston.

They talked about names. The man suggested Mitchell, after a younger brother who'd died. But Coreen wasn't sure.

"This boy ain't lucky as it is." She spoke softly, but didn't mumble. "I can feel it in my bones."

Bea heard something in Coreen's voice that she hadn't before. Or maybe, she thought, she was hearing Coreen's voice just as it was.

"Never mind your bones," the boyfriend said, laughing. "All you women, nothing you like better than worrying. Hell, we got us a son! Come to Daddy, little Mitchell! First thing's gonna happen now your daddy's come back, he's gonna buy you some pants!"

Coreen's fever returned, no one knew why. The doctors spoke to her kindly, but they said she couldn't leave. She told them her twins were only three years old. She said she might lose her job. Precisely, they said, what she needed was rest, which she wouldn't get at home.

In the middle of the night, though she must have felt ill, Coreen changed her baby's diaper for the third or fourth time. Then she rang for the nurse.

"Look at these diapers! You tell me his shit's supposed to be *red*."

"Oh!" Patrice said. Bea heard the nurse's shoes slap the linoleum as she ran down the hall. She returned with a doctor whose voice Bea didn't recognize. He had a rich, soothing accent—English, or Australian. He paused between phrases as if to gauge the responses of someone whose reactions might be different from his.

He was... concerned, he told Coreen, that her son might have... a serious form of diarrhea. An infection in the bowel. Not so rare, really, especially for babies like hers... premature. They were taking him to Children's Hospital, just down the street. She could see him as soon as... she was feeling "more perky." In the meantime, he said, they'd send word... how he was.

An orderly wheeled the child out the door. Bea thought of pushing through the curtain to comfort Coreen, but what could she say? That the doctors at Children's were the best in the world? That she hadn't broken her promise not to let them take him?

Early the next morning Bea dressed herself, then her son. Bundled in the snowsuit Bea's mother had sent him, Isaac seemed thoughtful, as if contemplating this change in his life. She took a deep breath and pushed aside the curtain, holding the gift her colleagues had sent; she had eaten one pear, but the rest of the pyramid of fruit was intact. She waited for her roommate to say *Keep your damn apples*. But Coreen didn't move her eyes from the woman in sequins spinning a huge shiny wheel on TV.

Bea set the fruit on the night stand. "I hope you feel better soon. I hope your baby is all right." She tried not to wish that her roommate would thank her. "Is there anything I can do?"

Coreen turned to face her. For some reason, Bea thought that her roommate would tell her to pray. But Coreen shook her head no and turned back to the spinning wheel on TV.

From the moment Bea came home she had no trouble nursing. She locked the doors and pulled the shades down. She peeled off

Isaac's diaper, T-shirt, and hat and gave him a bath. Seeing him naked and whole the first time she felt a catch in her throat, a pressure in her chest. She assumed this was love, but the word seemed too weak, as if she'd grown up calling pink "red," and then, in her thirties, seen crimson or scarlet.

Isaac slept by her side. Whenever he was hungry she gave him a breast. Milk spurted in his mouth so quickly it choked him; she had to pump out the excess, which sprayed from each nipple like water from a shower head. He would suck half an hour at each breast, if she let him. How could she watch his face for so long and still not be bored? Perhaps if she observed him closely enough she would be able to determine the instant at which pure matter, pure flesh, was transformed into mind.

Her elation, she knew, was due to a hormone. But who would have thought that a chemical substance could produce this effect? If vials of oxytocin could be bought at a store, who would drink or use drugs? She hadn't suspected that of all the emotions a human being could feel, this...tenderness...would be the one she craved most.

When she felt a bit stronger Bea telephoned the hospital and asked a nurse in obstetrics if Coreen Jones had gone home. Yes, she had, the nurse said. And her baby? Bea asked. "Just a moment," the nurse said. A few minutes later she got back on the line and said that the baby had been transferred to Children's, that was all the information she could release at this time.

When she called Children's Hospital, Bea introduced herself as Dr. Beatrice Weller, which was technically true. She learned that a patient listed only as "male infant Jones" had died two days earlier. She said, "Yes," and hung up.

That afternoon she borrowed a pouch from the family next door, strapped Isaac inside it, and walked to the T. As she stood by the turnstile, struggling to get some change from her pocket, someone behind her said, "Honey, don't rush. What a mother really needs isn't a pouch, it's an extra pair of hands."

The woman who'd said this was at least six feet tall, with soft, sculpted hair and perfect brown skin. She wore a yellow cashmere suit and enormous brass earrings. Bea wondered if she might be one of the anchors on the local evening news, then decided that such a celebrity wouldn't be taking the T.

The woman dropped a token in the box for Bea's fare. Bea tried to repay her. The woman lifted one palm. "Pass it on, pass it on."

Before Bea could answer, the woman pushed through the gate and, briefcase to chest, ran to catch her train.

When Bea got to the hospital she went straight to Room 3. She said she'd come to buy a picture for a friend who was ill, wrote a check for twenty dollars, and was handed a portrait in a flimsy pink folder with bears at one edge. Clipped to the front was the form they'd filled out: MOTHER'S NAME... ADDRESS...Coreen's writing was shaky; Bea remembered her leaning on the woman in front.

She opened the folder. Yellow pinafore with ruffles. Curls. Pursed, full lips. She thought of mailing the portrait, but decided to follow through with her plan. To hand a person an envelope and offer your condolences for the death of her child seemed a minimum requirement for living on earth.

She took the subway to a neighborhood she'd never been to before. The three-decker houses weren't all that much different from the ones where she lived, but the smallest details—a pair of red sneakers dangling from a telephone wire, an unopened pack of gum lying in a gutter—seemed enlarged and mysterious. Most of the houses were enclosed by steel fences. German shepherds and Dobermans strained at their leashes and barked as she passed. With her cheek to Isaac's soft spot she could feel his brain pulse.

She found the building at last. Three rusty mailboxes hung askew on the porch, an eagle on each: HERRERO, GREEN, JONES. Had she really believed she could ring Coreen's doorbell and explain why she'd come? When Coreen saw the photo of her dead son, she would scream, perhaps even faint. Besides this, Bea knew, she was holding a healthy baby in the pouch on her chest, and that, more than anything—her job, or her color, what she did or didn't say—would make Coreen hate her.

A light flickered on behind a third-story window. She pictured Coreen lying on her bed, stone mute with grief. Her boyfriend came in. *Don't worry, sweetheart, we'll have another baby. It wasn't your fault.* Bea wondered where the twins were. And Lena? Coreen's mother? What about her job? Would they allow her time off? How useless the eye without the imagination to inform it, to make sense of the darkness surrounding the light.

A child started crying in the building next door. Bea's breasts began to tingle; in his pouch Isaac stirred. She bent the folder slightly and slid it in the mailbox. Milk flowed from her nipples, soaking her blouse. She hurried to the T station, where she zippered her parka so that only Isaac's head poked from the top.

Her last night in the hospital she had lain with her hands pressed to her ears as Coreen changed her baby's diaper again and again. By then Bea herself had come down with a fever. Every joint ached. Her breasts had swollen grossly. They were lumpy, rock hard, as if someone had pumped them full of concrete. Another few drops and they would burst, or they'd shatter.

And yet they kept filling. Each time Coreen's baby whimpered, milk surged into Bea's breasts, pushing through ducts that felt tiny and clogged, like irrigation ditches silted with clay. In another few moments she would be forced to get up and stagger down the hall and try to stop Patrice from feeding Isaac the formula she had warned she would give him. Bea longed to feel his mouth sucking her nipples, sucking and sucking, easing her pain. In the meantime she lay there, palms to her ears, breasts filling with milk for another woman's child.

Tzimtzum: Contraction

The contractions
    Have come
Too soon   You are sentenced

    To bed   in the country house

During the tedious hours
Your sons scrap   Your husband courts
An imaginary lover   You summon

    the living Mothers:

        Hagar
            Of the bitter smile
        Sarah
            Whose laughter lies
        Rebecca
            Who outwits men
        Leah Rachel
            Phantom beauties

In such company you lie
Opposed to
Gravity that would steal
The new one   prematurely

Who brushes   your hair
Who prepares   grains
Who rubs   the mirror clear
    These attendants

And on the Sabbath
Your men   like an Austrian forest
Close around you   tall dark green

You sing   *N'sh*   *n'sham*   *n'shama*

Till the eyes close

Come, now, new one
Ride the waters
Into your mother's arms
Fill these woods with a cry

Note: Rabbi Aryeh Kaplan writes, "The word Tzimtzum *means 'constriction' [or contraction], and refers to the process by which God 'withdrew' His light in order to create the universe."* N'shama *is one of the Hebrew words for soul.*

Physics

after Stephen Hawking

Jimmy Alvarez and Emilio Sanchez and his brother
are absent forever,
each shot in the head in the park,
and so their membership has lapsed with the Latin Kings.

Slumped in their car seats,
they look as if they drank too much
except that their lips are frosted white
over pearl and blood,
as they pass away under the autumn stars,
stars so clear that they reveal primary colors
of age and power.

Jimmy's girl, Maria, and his daughter walk out
past the baseball diamond
into the field,
then away together
into teenage grief.

                 If only the three could wake,
they'd brush off the safety glass pooled in their laps
and swing open the car doors
into the question of before and after,
into the extinguished world.

But this is where the expanding universe collapses
for each individual,
and in the collapse
each life is played in reverse—

Jimmy Alvarez and Emilio Sanchez and his brother
climb back into the Camaro,
bullets fly back into their chambers,
and they are joined up again
before the betrayal of the Latin Kings.

Instead of withdrawing himself from Maria's body,
Jimmy enters her again.
Sperm floods back into his body
as if to make himself fertile,
as if to go back to blinding source of desire
in the proven world
of spirit and brotherhood.

The Weight of Memory

When they were still young
and love
was not yet their protection,
he fell,
though only once, into what he called
another woman's arms.

But she understood him, and
speaking the language of betrayal,
she understood him to mean
another woman's legs,
and it was this understanding
she was trying to swallow.

> *If I could make this pain small,*
> *small enough to fit the palm*
> *round like a donut, I could*
> *swallow it then, erase it*
> *in a single bite.*

Yet somehow,
even when the donut was gone
the hole remained,
she could feel it
moving from her mouth
to her throat and on, until

it came finally to rest
in the space below her ribs.
Her husband saw it there,
could feel the groove

between her breasts,
growing deeper.

> *The hole you're trying to fill*
> *is only widening your hips,*
> *this is my mistake, yet your*
> *legs are becoming*
> *another woman's*

What he did not know
is that they were
already,
his wife coming to carry
not only her own legs
but the hips, the thighs of the other.

> *My skin stretches.*
> *She lives with me*
> *here*
> *every day*
> *and sometimes he makes love*
> *not to me*
> *but to my*
> *her*
> *legs*

She carried this,
the weight of memory
as we carry the dead with us,
a burden of flashback
to suddenly be
somewhere else,

seeing things
never seen, things
he might have said,
thinking what he might think

carrying always these two weights
like a stone on each shoulder:

the knowing,
the not knowing.

The Human Voice

All night rain ran down the window
in the spare bedroom where I slept; outside,
the lime tree's runneled leaves absorbed
wave after wave of the Pacific storm,

which, like a riot, had been pre-
dicted by the authorities; awake
in the smallest hour, I heard
a woman's voice rise and join the weather—

my friends making love, their house
an instrument to amplify desire.
I wished them joy, marriage being
the hardest art I know of, and the least

certain of success. As I fell
asleep a voice rose from an alleyway
where I'd first heard it years before
in Fez, of a husband keening for his wife:

His fingers stroked the skin of dust
on the paving stones, ransacking their surface
for some comfort, knowing that
her body would be carried to the hills

it was just possible to see
from that place, where it would be laid beneath
the trees and sprinkled with lime,
to burn away the flesh. To sing.

True Prophets

Their speech doesn't sound prophetic: "Wish the damn heat
would let up." "Do you carry three-inch finishing nails?"
Too late their wisdom becomes clear. True prophets,

though, care nothing for prophecy. It just sweats out
of them like garlic from the pores of one who eats
Korean food. Prophets adore food which is thoughtfully

prepared. Sometimes at a restaurant, a prophet will leap
from his chair shrieking with rage, or laugh for no apparent
reason, or weep uncontrollably. The latter response

indicates a profound meal. Prophets will speak of it
for centuries, and congregate where it was served, although
it rarely reoccurs. Prophets love billiards, too, but play

badly. Whatever sparks their gift robs them of any sense
of angles or geometry. They can play hours without
sinking a ball. When one goes in—even the white—

every prophet on earth feels an orgasmic shudder.
Sex does not interest prophets. Perhaps knowing
the outcome makes them lackadaisical. This may explain

their rarity; they mate infrequently, and never
with the same person twice. The offices of marriage
counselors are relatively full of prophets, though

this fact does prophet-seekers little good. What most
upsets a prophet is the so-called "hot foot,"
in which matches are stuck between the sole and upper

of a shoe, then lit, causing the victim to dance
wildly, and if the victim is a prophet, to fall
into a trance from which he or she can only

be awakened by a rap on the "funnybone."
With the advent of tennis shoes, however,
and migration of the populace toward video games,

MTV, and shopping malls, this method of "turning
a prophet," like prophets themselves, has ceased
to have any significance at all.

Surrounded

There are no albums of family photographs in our house. Before he left last Sunday night, Gort must have carried them all out the front door and piled them at the curb for the garbage men. The black marbled copybooks full of nature notes must have gone the same way; when I broke into the safe on Tuesday it was empty.

There was one album that he left behind—I never got around to fitting any photographs into it. Every night now, while Susie sleeps in her crib upstairs, I sit in the dark living room with a glass of brandy on the floor beside me and this green padded album in my lap. I listen to the summer night: the bleat of an ambulance; the splintery crash of bottles being hurled into the recycling bin on the corner; the seesaw pulsing of the crickets. I turn the empty pages one by one.

RED LIPSTICK, 1981

All eyes are on them—the couple at the top of the aisle, waiting for the organist to find her sheet music. *Cousins shouldn't marry:* the eyes moving speculatively over the bride's satin-covered stomach hold visions of babies with missing limbs, or too many. The couple stand side by side with their arms linked and their eyes on each other. Her father has declined to give the bride away. No one will give her; she will give herself.

The groom is pale in the formal black cutaway he uses for work (he's putting himself through M.I.T. as a free-lance pallbearer); his damp, ginger-ale hair is combed sternly back. He cannot stop smiling. The bride wears a yellowed satin gown from another time, the gown in which her favorite aunt married a cruel man she has luckily outlived. The bride, too, is pale, except for the bright slash of her mouth, the deepest shade she could find in Walgreen's, brighter and deeper than blood.

The mother of the bride lays a hand on one satin sleeve. The organ sounds its first long interrogatory note.

SURROUNDED, 1982

Birds on the roof wake her—the click of their feet across the shingles, like her mother's old treadle sewing machine. There is a heavy, sweet smell. She lifts her head from the damp crook of her arm. There are lilacs everywhere. By her cheek, in the triangle between her belly and her pulled-up legs, along her naked back. She rolls over. A broken-off branch jabs her spine. Sitting up, she wraps her arms around her legs. Her own flesh comforts her, the creamy feel of her breasts against her bare knees. There are lilacs heaped on the tangled army blankets at the foot of the bed, lilacs arranged in a row along each side. The breeze through the open window carries the late afternoon voices of children.

He appears in the doorway then. Catholic funerals last longer— two hours this time—and they don't pay you extra. He didn't mean it, what he said, before.

Afterwards she holds him, still in his scratchy black jacket, in her arms. The smell of crushed flowers is all around them, a gobbling sweetness, sweet as laughter. They listen to the noise on the roof. Gort says, "Birds in galoshes."

FIRE! GOODBYE, 1984

The new house faces north, toward the lights of Boston, with relics of previous owners rusting in the yard. In the midnight kitchen—she forgot to have the electricity turned on—streetlights show cartons piled on the floor beside the new kitten's bed, on the old mouse-colored linoleum countertops, on the round table. Gort, standing naked at the telephone, chews the skin of his lower lip.

She holds up one of the cue cards she's made for these calls from Albert, Gort's boss at Woods Hole, who's taken to phoning late at night with long incomprehensible stories of attack and pursuit. She points a flashlight and clicks it on. *More in Morning! Goodbye.*

Outside, rain is falling, serious and slow, filling the cellar with sooty brown water. She holds up another card. *Someone at Door! Goodbye.* Gort shifts the phone to his other ear and leans against a laundry basket filled with dishes. Lightning cracks outside. She can see the movement of his lungs against the thin ribs. His bony shoulders curve forward; his penis in its shadowed nest of hair trembles lightly. She shines the flashlight on her last card.

EGG, 1984

In another room, the baby cries. Shouting, the woman picks up an egg. The baby cries; the egg strikes the edge of the counter next to the man's clenched hand, slides down the white painted cabinet, pools on the floor. The yolk is bright yellow. They look at each other, appalled; then, at the same moment, they start to laugh.

The man crouches and begins collecting pieces of eggshell. He piles the shards carefully on his palm, as if they could be reassembled later.

THE ROSE-COLORED UMBRELLA, 1987

Autumn is late this year. It's still warm enough for a barbecue, though red dogwood and pin oak and maple leaves have been drifting down all afternoon, and the catalpa in the back corner of the yard is already bare. Gort sits in the wooden porch swing with his three-year-old daughter. He holds the hard little heels of Lil's bare feet, one in each hand. On the steps his nephew, Daniel, sits turning the pages of the Bird Book, in which they recorded that morning, out of season, a dark-eyed junco. Gort sings,

> *You're my little potato*
> *You had wrinkles*
> *On the bottom of your feet*

Under the catalpa Judith piles handfuls of silverware into a blue bowl. The paper plates with their crust of baked beans she shuffles into a green plastic garbage bag held open by her brother-in-law, James. They wipe the wooden table with paper napkins.

They close the faded canvas umbrella for the season.

Before they turn to walk away, James puts the palm of his hand against the slope of her belly. He says, "Your eyes are a beautiful color in this light." He says, "Blue amber eyes." Silent, not knowing any reply, she watches chickadees pick over leaves on the grass; an iridescent black fly lands on a coil of dogshit. Her main feeling is surprise: he must know that she doesn't want—has never wanted—anyone but his brother. But James sleeps with everybody—ugly, irresistible James.

When she looks back from the porch, James is still standing by the dusty rose umbrella, like the folded wings of a huge moth, with the leaves glittering and falling all around him. Beside her, Gort rests his chin on Lil's head.

> *You're my little potato*
> *You come*
> *From underground*

ALLEY OF THE MOON, 1989

They've been driving through rainy fog for six hours, seven, over narrow roads that run alongside dim November fields. Then trees—maple, oak, hickory, paper birch, fir and pine and spruce—their colors muted as if under water. The inside of the car, newly shampooed for this, their last trip to the lake until spring, smells like Juicy Fruit. She feels as if someone had clapped a nose cone over her face and held it there. Her jaw aches from yawning.

By the time they get through Dayville, it is dusk. Elbow Lake is still an hour away. The sun, wherever it is, has set; the sky is as blank as the highway, they run together, broken only by the occasional greasy lights of an oncoming car.

"We'll have to stop." Gort flexes his fingers on the sky-blue steering wheel. He hates fog: the blankness where the headlights end, having to take on faith what's beyond. "Visibility's too bad."

Judith hides her gladness and peers with a concerned forehead through the windshield. Gort loves the lake, the land their shared grandfather bought in the middle of the Depression, a high wooded bluff where two lakes meet. She hates the lake, or fears it;

maybe both. Not the endless mutter of water, the canvas tent struggling against the tent pegs, the mildew-tasting fish; it's something else, something she can't name.

The blurred sign for the Valley of the Moon Motel—one long contorted tube of green light with its first letter extinguished—is so large they can see it from the road. They park between bare bushes spiked with red berries. Through an uncurtained window they can see a man behind a counter looking out. He is large—not fat, but wide—in a faded flannel shirt, with pale skin and hair nearly but not quite white.

Gort goes into the tiny office, talks to the wide-chested man, comes out. She cranks the window down and the car fills with the smell of wet bark and kerosene. Gort touches her hair, frizzed up from the fog like Easter-basket grass. "Be right back." He walks away down the narrow cement walk bordered by a row of identical blue doors. The fog opens to take him in. He disappears.

She waits. Five minutes? Ten? Underneath the motel's name a white worm of light says *Eat. Rest.* She has no watch. On the wall behind the motionless motel keeper the arrow-shaped hands of a clock point permanently at noon. Or midnight. She misses five-year-old Lil, the warm steadying weight of her body.

It's absurd to be afraid. There's the motel sign's soupy light, the wide window, the bright anonymous beam of the motel keeper's eyes. But for the first time and quite without warning, she knows. She understands that all of it exists just here, just now: a narrow band between blankness and blankness, a moment without past or future.

BLANK PAGES

In one of the bare spots every album has (always more frequent towards the end), Gort buys a small black safe at the Sussex Hotel's liquidation sale and installs it in the unfinished half of the attic, for his copybooks. The lists Judith has gotten used to finding around the house—between the hammock pillows, on the back of the grocery list, under his place mat at the kitchen table—include more and more items that don't belong. *Original Sin(?).* *Coelacanthus in 1938. Go to Russia.* Small things, and none of it seems *real;* and he is more often simply the person he always was. The good lover; the good father. Lil seems to know how to comfort him. For the time being, Judith decides, it is enough to be watchful.

JUST TWO GUYS, 1992

In Lil's eighth summer, a new baby appears. They call her Susie, a foolish, frilly name, in Lil's opinion. Her father, who is always sad now, says, "Fishing, Lil," and "Just the two of us"; and they get in the old blue Dodge and go. Gort wears a red Phillies cap, and his girl, who everyone says is the image of her father, wears one, too. They leave the womenfolk (there are two now) behind.

At sunset the frogs make a sound like rubber bands. Lil stands on a thick, alligator-skinned limb halfway up a big cedar; its trunk grows out of the bluff at a slant, almost horizontal over the lake. Farther out, the lake doubles the trees around its edge: pine and hemlock and silver birch. Naked except for her puffy orange water wings, she looks down through the cedar fronds. The shallow water is clear and green with purple-shadowed depths. She holds onto a branch near her head and watches for the flicker of sunfish where the water darkens.

A bluejay lands at the end of the limb. Its beak opens. Lil can see the black tongue inside. She looks straight down into the water and spits. It marks the surface with a distant dimple, like a water strider. She laughs; the bird flies off.

"Daddy. Hey, Dad!" She turns back to where her father, one shoulder hunched, moves slowly between the green canvas tent and the fire with its thin flag of smoke. "Daddy, look! Watch *this!*"

He looks up then. His face is full of sunset light.

She jumps.

IN THE BATHROOM, 1992

Just tell me where you go, that's all. I just need to know where you *are.*

Out. I go out.

Gort. Please.

Gort.

Christ, Jude. Will you leave me alone, for once. For *once,* would you just not ask me.

Are you. Is there. Do you have somebody else?

Oh, for Christ's sake.

If you would just. You're so *quiet* all the time—

Don't. Don't. Look, your glasses'll get all steamed up. Here.

I can't help it.

Judith. Please.

Jude— Okay.

Where are you going?

Out.

FOR ONCE, 1993

Without his glasses, Gort's face looks nude; you can see one eye turn slightly inward. He's sitting on the bare wood floor in the unfinished half of the attic, next to his rumpled sleeping bag, legs stretched out in front of him. By his feet is an empty white porcelain pot. The skylight above his head holds a dim winter sun, a few maverick snowflakes. His telescopes stand in a corner, pointed at the floor. The lens of the larger one is cracked straight across.

She sits on her heels next to the chamber pot holding Lustyka, the cat, in her arms for warmth. Gort starts to speak, falls silent, starts again. He doesn't look at her, but at the bare feet protruding from his blue pajamas.

Whatever it is, it's better left unsaid. Her terrible aloneness is all she has left of Lil. She no longer wants to—can't afford to—share it. And so "Hush," she says, "hush, it's all right," though nothing will ever be right again, and moves over to him. He smells like milk gone bad. She pulls his head down into her lap. Pliable as a rag doll, he lies with his head next to the cat's rump, his legs and buttocks still sitting.

Rumbling softly, Lustyka starts to wash herself. The pink triangle of tongue makes its way slowly along her haunches and into Gort's thick, pale hair. Judith looks up at the skylight and wishes she were out there, floating free—or that he were. For a long time they sit like that, in silence, with snow zigzagging in the cold sun and the cat's tongue rummaging tenderly through Gort's hair.

The noises of the city have quieted. The stop-and-start sound of the crickets has stopped for good. I close the album, my hands trembling only a little now. A scrapbook: scraps. I can move things here and there, arrange them however I like. That's the advantage of everything being gone. I lick the skin of brandy from the bottom of the glass. Then I lock up and go to bed and lie in the dark listening for the soft thud of plaster falling from the ceiling.

He told me once about the ancient tribes who may have crossed over to this continent from Asia on the ice sheet and slowly found their way down the coast. An era ended, and the ice sheet melted. The level of the ocean rose. The trail was lost.

La Source

to Grandmother,
Port-au-Prince, Haiti,
August 1991

I bear down on the leaf
that carries me to home and ground,
peer through a corner,
see
the gaze that slipped in and out of walls at home,
bared,
looking at the valley,
a brown wind that uncords knots,
binds storms to dust,
lifts stars,
skies,
the abscess from my eyes.
I have left the eighteen floors,
the glass
that divides and dries;
I am her
with my
slanted, sideways glances.

I am six,
Grandmother,
the source,
on the hilltop,
on the way to Kinscoff,
her light's medulla more than a halo.
She splits a pomegranate open with her blaze,
seeds spore
and birth beyond her arms' embrace,
beyond the tremblings that rocked her days.

I return,
to see
her reach other arms:
her land—
the mango, the mapou, the hoe,
the red earth rank with ants,
chasing one another in a maze
(the haze of summer does not deter them);
the pigs squabble beside her outhouse,
while she sits on the terrace
watching
the neighbor turn her eyes inside out
as a lizard stings them with its tongue.

Climb up the road to Turgeau,
you will find her.
Past the cemetery.
La Source,
you will find her.

Building Fence

My brother, my son, they're setting
jack posts, stringing wire in high wind.
I come after, pounding staples in good
pine wood. We follow the edge of the jack pine
where the foothill opens out to long drop
after drop of tough grass sliding down
the Front Range. We know it's a fine day,
a rare day, our banter raucous, intent,
tossed to the wind. We're cold, hungry,
but set to get the work done.

My brother could always get something
done. Rebuilt that old Chevy he'd
broke down right to the screws. First
day he had it working, he gave our dad
a ride on the chassis, scattered gravel
as they chugged the road. Then my brother
learned to put people back in their bones
whole, when before they'd only been
painful parts. And his fishing is legend.
He taught that to my son.

My son could catch fish in the clearest
waters, enough to feed the whole bunch
hunkered down to plates and forks. Early,
he built a whole from parts—heard people's
scattered stories, wove the fragments
together. Then, his listeners could hold
their present in the hands of their history.
And very young, he wanted to know of earth,
of lives lived on it.

When I drive the old road in sight of
that fence, now, I know that another
fine day, rare day, there'll just be
my brother ahead of me setting posts.
I don't know why my son should die
a young man before he could get done
what he wanted. I only know to thread
that day's green needles through me,
bring back what we all got done together
one wind-loud day on the Front Range
looking east, never worrying west. More than
two hundred staples that day to my credit. No count
for my loss to grass.

Melissa's Abstract

Magpie calls bounce off the brittle
branches flaring off the mountain's
dark. One's wing just flew across
the branch tips. Just the banner of himself
he drew across. His darkness cast a kind
of laugh against the brilliance of the
icy bark.

I remember iced branches out our window
fifteen, sixteen years ago an ocean away from here.
You painted them in brightest flailing shards
of red black blue and, yes, hard green.

Not the realistic scene, your art teacher
in that small island school said. The one
you should have seen out our window. You
told us with puzzled dismay, without rancor.

I can still look through that stone squared
window our first winter morning above the sea,
still hear our words pluck at the art teacher's
plight. Just the banner of sardonic selves
we flaunted in that hour.

If Earth Is One of Seven

If Earth is one of seven
ancient
wandering stars,
where is that girl who, every afternoon,
    runs water into a basin of hollow scales?

Surely not in the vertical crowds,
among colonizers and women passing in shallow hats.
Nor riding with the plutonium makers, without hair or
   explanations,
    whose buckles glow in the dark.

Even today,
bottles are blasted in furnaces, thrown behind pillars.
In this plague year, water saplings are seen at the edge of the
   lagoon,
fluids draining from us. All of us related,
    all of us accused.

The directions lead through unclaimed streets,
    an earthly mourners' route. Not Venus, Jupiters, Mars.
Not Mercury or Saturn with its promissory rings.
Let that girl go on washing the bandages.
Let her blow softly on the tightening scars,
    the persistent reminders.

1-800-HOT-RIBS *Poems by Catherine Bowman. Gibbs Smith, $9.95 paper. Reviewed by Diann Blakely Shoaf.*

RISE THE EUPHRATES *A novel by Carol Edgarian. Random House, $22.00 cloth. Reviewed by Don Lee.*

THE OPEN BOAT: POEMS FROM ASIAN AMERICA *An anthology edited by Garrett Hongo. Anchor Books, $12.00 paper. Reviewed by Stewart David Ikeda.*

A BRIEF HISTORY OF MALE NUDES IN AMERICA *Stories by Dianne Nelson. Univ. of Georgia Press, $19.95 cloth. Reviewed by Jessica Dineen.*

At the Cass Lake E-Z Stop, I find
a T-shirt pinned to the wall.
Where Eagles Soar.

I don't remember eagles here,
just my father saying, *God,
look how they live*

as we passed through,
four kids and a dog
in the back seat of a Buick.

Eagles, hawks, doves.
I never quite understood the stories.
From around here, the Bear Clan.

*Like the bear, we scare people.
Scared ourselves, we turn
and run into the woods.*

I buy the T-shirt with its awful
green lettering. It's what I know.
Purchase. Surrender.

Snowfield

The last deportations from the town in Poland where my father had been born, and where his parents lived, were carried out in October 1942. The town was declared *Judenrein*. This word was written in the center of the green ruled page that my father found when he returned to Poland after the war. It was the only German word in the book. There was a date: 21.6.42. A fourteen-page list of names, addresses, and ages preceded this date. The last name was Tadeusz Mitwocz. My father had returned to Poland to look for his parents. Their names were on the eleventh page.

In 1942 my father lived in New York. He had met my mother there, in a bookstore where she worked most evenings. That was 1933. The owner of the bookstore allocated only so many dollars a month to heating; when that was spent, he turned it off. My father was attracted to the long black stockings my mother wore, which were as dark as her hair and accentuated the flat, clouded white of her exposed wrists and slim neck. He sat on a footstool in his coat and hat to read what he could not afford to buy. He lied to her about where he lived, because he did not want to explain why he walked past the warm library to get to this cold bookstore. "How's your friend Towshtoy today?" she would ask him, mimicking the accent that I never heard. He had meticulously eliminated all trace of it by the time I was old enough to recognize foreign English. She stole books for him sometimes. She was from Chicago. She had seen Jews, and waited on them, but never known one. And he was nearly ten years older than she. But they were married in January 1934. That November I was born. In 1942 they separated, and my mother moved back to Chicago, taking me with her. Despite a freeze order on civilian passenger service, my father had the means to allow me to ride the train back to New York to visit.

For two years I traveled with a woman named Constance Martin, whom my mother had found in the newspaper. She stayed with her brother and his family in Queens over the long weekends I spent with my father. To my parents she referred to herself as a "governess," but to me she claimed to be a "travel partner," though she slept through as many as twelve of the fifteen hours we spent on the train. We rode the New York Central's *Pacemaker,* an all-coach liner, so that Mrs. Martin had to accommodate herself in the tall-backed, red upholstered banquette, despite the fact, she said, that my father could certainly afford a Pullman berth for us on the *Lake Shore Limited.* She said, "I don't blame your poor mother. But look at me. I'm light-headed. The blood pools in my bottom from sitting up at night. You wait until you're my age."

She repeated these same words every trip, in her floating, oversized voice. I thought she had a bad memory. She spoke with her head turned partway between myself on the banquette beside her and the people facing us opposite. She kept her eyes on the window but did not seem to see through it. She said, "Such an important Jewish man—your father. One should think he might spare some of those means on his family."

While she slept I walked between the cars that were full of men in uniform. The trains became crowded again during the war, and sometimes there was an antique wooden coach filling out the middle of the line. These had stained glass windows and a hopper in the bathroom—you could see the tracks skimming by. It was hard to imagine the quiet yards where these cars had sat quiet for so long.

We left the La Salle Street Station at 5:20 and traveled to New York primarily through the dark, especially in winter. The windows became black and empty between Gary and Toledo, and again between Toledo and Cleveland, where the track was perfectly straight for over one hundred miles. The day coaches were full of sleeping bodies. Sometimes the quiet made them seem empty. There were children my age who sat still and awake beside their parents. We stared at each other. The lounge car startled me with its loud busyness and laughter. I never lingered there. I kept my eyes on the carpet. At the front of the train, the baggage car came directly behind the engine, "So you-all don't hit first in case a crash," the porter told me. He was fat. He guarded the door. No one was allowed in the baggage car, but when I stood still before him long enough he asked if I wanted a peek. There were only four windows inside. The moon lit four pools of gray and in these pools the full rows of tiered shelving formed vague, bulky shapes. The porter took the flashlight from his belt. He pointed it across a row of green duffel bags and green numbered trunks, interspersed by a stray blue or beige suitcase. "Lots of fresh bodies," the porter said. "No bones this trip, but a whole lot of fresh bodies." I looked for my suitcase but did not see it.

Each time, my father sent a different woman to pick me up at Grand Central. I learned to identify them before they approached: overdressed women with dramatic hats and pained expressions, lackadaisically searching the passengers along the ramp, hanging back behind the crowd, smiling late when they recognized my father in me. Mrs. Martin relinquished me to them unwillingly. But I looked forward to their smells, and their hats, and their sheer-stockinged legs crossed at the knee in the cab. I liked the way they looked beside my taller, older father and his black hat. I couldn't feel threatened by their jealous attempts to horde his attention because I had known him long enough to understand that neither of us had a chance. I wanted to warn these women sometimes—when they were good to me—but I didn't know how. Sometimes it made me sad to see a new woman on the platform. I wondered what had happened to the last.

All day Saturday, and also on Monday, I tagged along with these girlfriends of his—shopping, visiting other bored and lovely women, waiting in the finest apartments in the city for the return of busy men, or sometimes, though not as often as expected, for their soldiers. I accompanied them to salons and dress shops and the offices of various doctors. I was surprised by the time required to maintain their casual, elegant appearances. Sometimes the cabs we rode would pass through Union Square into the neighborhood where my mother had lived when she came to the city. We never traveled on the piece of 16th Street where her apartment was because the block dead-ended into Stuyvesant Square: a seminary and the little park. But I knew when we were close and I was able to remove myself from the cab and from the insubstantial woman beside me. My mother and I alone knew about this place, I thought—even my father had forgotten.

Finally, late in the evening, we might end up at the Club 18 on 52nd Street, where my father would hug me and laugh and dote. At our dark table in the buzzing room, with the fat jazz singer closing her eyes around the words and sleep taking me further from the conversation, I watched my father with these women, and with the well-dressed, younger men at our table. I felt that he was a person to be admired. He was a Bergsonite. They wanted to rescue the Jews, get them to Palestine. My father was going to make the British bomb the railroads in Poland. Those were different trains. We sat with other Bergsonites, and I listened alternately to their conversation and to the conversation of the women, who knew about the sad lives of the jazz singers we saw. Sometimes I closed my eyes. The woman with my father would say, "Your boy just turned out the lights, Josh. We should have got a sitter."

"He's not sleeping," my father said. I might smile but keep my eyes closed.

The woman said, "Oh no? Well, then maybe he's dead."

"It could be," my father said. "He's an old man. It will happen."

My smile would grow. She said, "But what if he's only drunk? We'd bury him alive, doctor." And he said, "We must tickle him, nurse. It's the only way to be sure." Then I would laugh and open my eyes. She would sit with her arm wrapped through his, her cheek against his shoulder. She would smile knowingly, reservedly. A thin smile.

Sunday afternoons my father spent alone with me—we walked in the park in any weather. He didn't mind if we got wet. He bought me strange trinkets at the museum gift shops: a pocket viewer with a photo of the city skyline, a gyroscope. I never knew what to do with his gifts. He had given me a gold necklace with a small gold star after I moved to Chicago. I didn't like the way it felt around my neck, but my mother made me wear it when I visited. She had cried when I showed it to her.

In 1944 I turned ten, and as promised, I was allowed to make the train trip alone. My mother and I did not speak about it. She had given me the ticket and I kept it in my dresser drawer beneath my socks. But that Thursday, during breakfast, she ran through a list of questions: What do I do if a stranger bothers me? Who do I talk to if I don't feel well? What if I don't see my father at the station? She was surprised at how well I knew my answers, as if she assumed that I had been asleep along with Mrs. Martin. She sat on my bed beside my suitcase while I packed and she made suggestions, but not many. She let me choose what I would wear for the train ride. Then she stepped back and looked at me, up and down, twirling her finger as if stirring ice in a glass. I turned around for her. It was a dark-green wool suit she had bought for my birthday. I liked the deep trouser pockets. My mother smiled when I was facing her again. She kissed her fingertips and opened them between us. "So old," she said. "You take care. I don't want any recruiter trying to sign my boy up just yet."

She left work early and met me at our apartment after school. Together we walked the seven long blocks to the station. The busy sidewalk by our building had been shoveled and trampled clear, but on South Clark Street it was reduced to a thin, icy path through the foot of snow on the ground. The sky threatened to dump more. At the station we had sandwiches from the vendor and I explained the difference between a trestle and a bridge to her. The *Pacemaker* was late—because of snow, we were told. I would return on Sunday, Christmas Eve, and my mother said we would have to rush to Union Station to catch the last commuter rail south to my grandmother's house. She said, "I don't suppose there are belated Chanukah plans on your father's end this year?"

"I don't know," I told her, though we had not celebrated Chanukah since I was five.

She nodded. "Does your father ever talk to you about God?" she asked. She never shied away from a question. It was a practice that had cost her some friends. But I liked it—I wanted to be asked difficult questions.

Lately, though, my father's letters had been brief and embarrassingly simple, as if I were still eight years old. Phone calls were strictly utilitarian and limited to three minutes. "No," I told her. "He doesn't."

She nodded again. She said, "He doesn't believe in God anymore. While we were married he lost his faith. You two have never talked about this?"

Then we heard the whistle and the train came into the station. "No," I told my mother, but she was looking at the train and didn't hear me. We counted cars: eleven day coaches, one Pullman ("For the trainmen," I said, though I was only guessing), a diner, and the baggage car. My ticket was for the third car back, one of those going all the way to New York. I thought my mother would continue our conversation, but she stood up from the bench and hugged me and we kissed. "Be good," she said. When I found my seat I waved to her through the pattern of frost on the window. She threw back a kiss. Then she turned and followed the passengers from New York streaming out of the station, which surprised me. I knew it would be half an hour or more before the train would depart, but I had expected her to wait on the bench, watching. I thought that I would be the one going away. She should be standing still.

It had begun to snow in the city when we pulled out, and it fell in slanted sheets between the rows of lit-up houses in Hammond. There was a soldier beside me in my berth. He was tall, as tall as my father. He was either nervous or excited—he couldn't sit still. Over and over he began to whistle the same tune, then cut himself off. It seemed to me that the old man and woman who shared the banquette across from us made him nervous. The woman had wide, thick-framed glasses that swallowed her eyes, but she seemed to stare alternately at the soldier and myself. I could not be sure, though. Whenever I dared to steal a glance, her gaze was directed absently at the wall between the two of us.

The old man's glasses made his eyes bug out, though I wondered if they were that way from his hard breathing. He breathed with his nose and his mouth at once—long breaths that sometimes ended in a wet cough and a labored swallow. He looked afraid. His shoulders sloped down into his chest, as if he were falling. I thought the woman should have been attentive to his cough, comforting him, and it seemed to me that the soldier thought the same thing.

Finally, in the midst of one of the man's coughing fits, the soldier sprang to his feet, startling me, and fled down the aisle. While I was gathering up the courage to follow him, the old woman said to me, "Are you traveling alone?" There was a note of disapproval in her voice, the phrasing of a teacher, so that I felt I had to sit still and answer.

I said, "Yes, ma'am."

"What's your name?" she asked, almost before I had answered.

"Stanley, ma'am."

"How old are you, Stanley? You can't be more than twelve."

The man beside her began a long gravelly cough. I waited for him to finish, trying to match the unwavering stare of the woman but unable to keep my eyes from the man. He held a handkerchief to his lips with both hands, and his wrists were corrugated with blue veins. The woman's stare was impatient.

Finally I said, "Ten years old."

"Well. Not so old. Have you been to New York before, Stanley?"

"Yes," I said. "My father lives there, ma'am."

"I see. Is your father a Jew, Stanley?"

I hesitated. Then I said, "Yes."

"He is." It was part question, part statement. "And your mother? He left her?" she asked.

I said, "No. My mother left him," though I didn't know if that was true.

"I see," she said again. "Sometimes little boys get adult things wrong, though. Don't they, Stanley? Your parents got out before Hitler, I suppose. Is that right? Maybe you're not sure."

I said, "Yes, ma'am."

"Well, good for them," she said. "God bless them."

The man beside her leaned farther forward, then swung slowly into a standing position. He began to shuffle between the woman and myself. She sat back out of his way, watched him pass. I said, "I have to go to the john." When the woman nodded, approving, I stood and followed the man.

I parted from him at the bathroom, where I locked the door behind myself and turned around to the sink. I washed my face, then lingered over my reflection in the mirror. My skin was pale against the dark green of my coat and the gold of my necklace. I made faces. I didn't have to wear a yarmulke, like some boys I had known in New York. For two years now I had been living with my mother, who was not Jewish. My father talked about the Jews, but he did not seem to act like one. I was becoming less and less Jewish. By the time I was an adult, I would be a Christian, like my mother.

In the bathroom was a tiny square window with a translucent pane of glass that could be slid open. If I stood on the toilet, I could just fit my head through the window. Outside the cold and the loud rhythm of the engine and the whine of the wheels were like the elements of another world. It was snowing—the snow fell across my face and into my eyes. The fields we cut through were dark and empty beneath the snow, with an irrigation ditch running close along the raised tracks. The blare of the train whistle startled me. We passed through an intersection where the bells and lights were everything for an instant, then gone behind us.

I walked through the train without seeing my soldier. Here and there were groups of men playing cards. In the coaches the groups were small and quiet, sometimes silent, but in the lounge car there was one large circle of men who were arguing and laughing at the same time. I went to the observation car at the back of the train. It had a rounded end full of windows where you could watch the tracks receding, and a glass ceiling as well. On clear nights all the stars were visible, but tonight it was just black. I could only see the snow falling through the shine of occasional street lamps. The streets were mostly empty. If I watched the track without taking my eyes from it, eventually it seemed as if it were moving, and the earth was spinning away from us. There was the loud clack and jerk when we crossed a switch point, then the other track would bend into or away from us.

When I returned to the berth the woman was asleep with her hands folded in her lap. The man had been looking out the window. He turned his scared eyes to me, then back to the window again. The soldier was still gone. I sat and watched the landscape go by, but this was the straight, empty stretch of track across the top of Ohio. I closed my eyes. The track was so straight here that the rock of the train between the rails became a slow, gentle drift. I listened to the man's large breaths. Soon I fell asleep. Outside the window the fields were white, but they slid away. The moon loomed large along the shoulder of a hill—it was bright in the empty snowfields. In the shadows. I heard the train whistle.

I was being shaken, a hand on my shoulder, and when I opened my eyes the soldier was there. "Psst," he said, jerking his chin toward the aisle in a "follow me" gesture. I was quiet, like him, because I thought the man and woman must be sleeping. But when I stood to follow I saw that the old man was awake and staring at me. I thought he might ask if he could come with us, but he didn't. He looked sad. He breathed as if it occupied his attention and his stare slipped down off of me.

I followed the soldier to the end of the car. He was tall, with the clipped black hair and a rolled cap hanging out of his pocket. He held open the door between cars and said, "You want to do me a favor, kid?"

He followed me now, with a hand on my back. He said, "I hope you weren't asleep." I shook my head no. He nodded. "Who could sleep in the sick berth back there?" He led me through the diner to the lounge car. "What's your name, anyway?"

"Stanley," I told him.

"You ever play cards, Stan?"

I nodded, though I hadn't.

"Good. You're not playing tonight but we need a banker over here. Our last banker had to go with his pop. You think you could be a banker?"

I nodded again.

"Where's your pop, Stan?"

"In New York," I said as we approached a table where four other men, all soldiers in identical uniforms, were sitting and laughing. My soldier stood behind me with his hands on my shoulders. He said, "Gentlemen," while they were still laughing. One by one, the four men turned to look at me. "Meet Stan the banker," he said.

The fat man across the table sat back so far in his chair that he seemed about to fall. He said, "A Jew, I guess. Leave it to Nate to find us a Jew banker."

There was laughter, and I blushed, while from behind me Nate said, "That so? Well, listen, Stan here is traveling alone. His old man's in New York."

"You a New Yorker?" one of the men asked. He wore glasses, and the lamp on the wall behind me covered them over in a reflected yellow glaze. I said, "Yes."

"That's good enough for me," he said. "Sit him down."

Nate brought me a Roy Rogers, which was what my father got me when we went to bars in New York. The man in glasses had a heap of bills separated into five clipped piles, each pile with a slip of paper on which a set of initials were written. He stacked the clipped piles into a single wad and rolled it into a green circle. He put a rubber band around that. Then he turned to me and stared for a moment, waiting, before he said, "Give me your hand, Stanley." Nate sat just on the other side of me. But he was occupied, talking to the fat man. I put my hand onto the table. The man in glasses took it into his hand. He put the money into my palm, then closed his two hands tight around mine. He stared at me again while he held my hand up between us, full of the money and enclosed in his own. He said, "Take this and put it into your underwear. You make sure it won't fall out. And you don't give anything to anybody unless I tell you to. All clear?"

He let go of my hand, but I sat still. Nate was still talking, gesturing toward the bar and laughing. I was alone with this man. He said, "In your underwear, Stanley." He motioned, holding his belt with one hand and pointing down along his belly with the other. "No joke."

I stood up. He put his hand around my arm, startling me. "Where you going, kid?"

"To the bathroom?" I said.

"No, no, no, no." He shook his head and held my arm, tightly. He said, "Loosen your belt. Go ahead. Here, put the money down for a minute. Now loosen your belt. Top button. There. In the underwear. Nobody's looking, Stanley, don't be shy." I did what he said. When I had buttoned my pants again he said, "Jump for me. Jump up and down for me."

I did. "It's not falling out?" he asked. I shook my head. When I had jumped, the money had settled into a lump at the bottom of my underwear, between my legs. It felt large and clumsy. I had to keep my legs spread slightly.

The man in glasses turned to the others and said, "Let's get going here." To me he said, "Sit down, Stanley. So far so good. All right?" I nodded. I knew from the tone of his voice that he could tell I was scared. But I didn't want him to speak sympathetically, or to apologize, because then I would cry. He said, "Relax now. You're a born banker."

Soon I did relax. Nate showed me his cards. I didn't know anything about the game, but I matched his facial expressions—pleased or not—and we pretended that I was helping. Sometimes he won on the hands that we had frowned at. They played with wooden chips. When the fat man wanted to leave, I had to take the damp, soft bills from my pants. The man in the glasses told me his initials and I found his bundle. Some of the money was returned to the fat man. The rest went back in my pants.

Then I watched them forget about me, something I was used to among adults, particularly in bars. The game became serious and they drank. Twice in a row the man in the glasses lost when the cards were shown. He swore and slammed his fist against the table. Then he was quiet, smoking, while the others talked between hands. I was not the only one who tried to ignore him. They talked about women and about women's names and about the places where these women lived. I became sleepy, but I did not intend to disappoint Nate as the banker before me apparently had. The train rocked beneath us, and I had the feeling that we were the only ones left awake apart from the engineer. Another man wanted to leave the game. "Cash him out," the man in glasses said to me. He told me the initials, then said, "Plus fifty-one." I didn't understand. Finally he took the money from me, annoyed, and paid the man. He said to me, "You short time this country? No learn math?"

I didn't answer. Nate shook the ice in his glass around in a circle and drank from it. The man gave me back the remaining bills. "Tuck 'em away," he said, and I thought he was done with me. But then he asked, "How old are you?"

"Ten," I said.

"Ten. Where the hell are your parents? Ten."

I didn't know if he wanted an answer. I began, "My father's..."

"Your father's in New York. Where's your mother?"

"Chicago."

"She a Jew?"

"No."

"Ah," he said, nodding, wagging a single finger. "Right. Yes.

Now I understand." I didn't know what he meant but I thought that I should, that it was something obvious. When the cards were dealt, the players became silent. In the middle of the hand, Nate asked me, "What does your old man do in New York, Stan?"

It was a question I had never learned how to answer. But since these men were soldiers, I thought they would understand if I told the truth. So I said, "He's making the British bomb the railroads in Poland."

"He's what?" the man in glasses asked.

"Is he in the service?" Nate asked.

I said, "No. He's a Bergsonite."

"He's a what?" The man in glasses began to laugh, which surprised me.

Another man said, "There's not many kids your age with a father around to visit these days." And the last man asked, "Are we playing cards here or what?"

But the man in glasses was still laughing. "A Bergsonite," he said, staring at me incredulously. "Is that some kind of secret Jew cult?" He leaned heavily into the table and held a hand out toward Nate, palm up. "What the hell is that?"

Nate shrugged. He said, "Let's play cards."

"A Bergsonite," the man said again, mimicking me. He laughed.

Later, when the game was over and I had returned to my berth and found some sleep, in the morning, in New York, the old man spoke to me in a quiet voice that was neither ghostly nor rasping, that I could not place with his menacing cough. He told me he had been in the old Grand Central in '88, during the storm. This was before they had switched to electric in the city. They fed the trains coal while they sat idle at the ramps. The steam warmed the building, and people came there from their frozen homes. "We slept over," the man said. "We couldn't get *out*. I'm seventy-four years old but I was a boy your age then. Oh, we slept on the floor, anywhere there was room. I was *sweating*, it was so warm. Two feet of snow. Imagine."

In 1948 my father married a Protestant woman from Long Island. My mother cried. "He lost his faith," she said. "Maybe it's my fault." I went to college in New York, and in a lecture on Zionism I learned who Peter H. Bergson was. The professor called him a terrorist. I tried very hard to avoid my father and his new wife at that time, but it was not always possible. They had two children—a girl and then a boy. My father said, "You were always your mother's child. I can't claim you." Later he said, "If your mother never left we would be happily married still." He died in 1964. Before he died he said, "All those trains you rode during the war, Stanley—comfortable, beautiful trains. I felt so guilty putting you on them." My mother never remarried. The older she got, the more she talked about my father. At his funeral she said, "You missed him—it's a shame. You were too young. During Passover he held a Seder in his tiny, dusty apartment. We ate bitter herbs. He recited from the Haggadah. You were four the last time he did this, Stanley. You don't remember? You stood on his lap and he held you. You spoke Polish with him—you knew a few words. This was before the war. He wanted to take us back there with him. He wanted to die in Poland then."

Nocturne for the Treaty Signing

Jerusalem, September 1993
for Raphi Amram

How long my hands
have been well-worn
thoughts of an automatic rifle.

Ajar,
my wrought-iron gate.
A mulberry tree, in leaf,
is shadowing the courtyard
tiles; the back of my hand
pouring wine's
caught in a dark pattern.

The walled Old City stares
across the valley, all luminous stone
like a white pomegranate
packed with ripe tears.
Life's brief,
hatred is fine
to abandon;

my garden quietly fills
with opening bars of music
broadcast from Jerusalem: the news.

Red Under the Skin

Seeing is forgetting the name of the thing one sees.
—Paul Valéry

The hatred goes back for centuries, everyone says,
        a tradition as old
                as making wine, weaving rugs, playing flutes.

    My father remarks
        he would have expected it
from the Croats
        who colluded with Hitler,
but not the loyal Serbs.

            Being Slovene makes him proud:

efficient factories, clean streets, their own language,

            independence.

    Forty years of exile, and he goes back
        and is proud.

                He never lost his accent.

When people ask me what I am,
    my friend Aida says, what am I to say?

Serbian Orthodox father.
Bosnian Muslim mother.
Croatian Catholic husband.

I used to call myself a Serb.

It was healing, you see, through intermarriage and friendship.

It WAS healing.

It was.

Now, nothing
she can do 6,000 miles away.

Or even there, what difference would it make?

One more death, like the husband of her best friend
who couldn't believe it, who walked out into the streets
of Sarajevo disbelieving, who was felled
by the first sniper bullets. Who cared
that he was a Serb married to a Muslim,
who had left Belgrade for love?
Now of course, he might be lucky,
lucky to have died.

Friends are cutting
her off, Aida says, because her family isn't *pure.*

Americans of Serbian or Croatian descent. Not recent emigrants,

but those like my father, who have been here for years.

It starts with rallies,
as in Belgrade in the fall of '88,
with Serbs chanting,

We are the victims of

The world is trying to extinguish

We will fight until

Like campaign buttons
        or bumper stickers. Nothing to be ashamed of
            letting the neighbors hear.
                Who was listening?

    In the Serb-Croatian War of 1991 (that war?
    war
        and more war)

the fiercest fighters were the émigrés,
      Croatians who returned
           from Canada or Australia or Germany
             or the U.S.

    to a land they knew only in the stories

of their parents.
             What were they told?

What the papers don't tell:
    Muslim, Orthodox, Catholic, Jew
        put up Christmas trees, exchanged gifts.

The Baptist on the plane asks me what denomination I am.

    His salary's tithed to Oral Roberts;
       his daughter has married a Palestinian
         whose fervor he can understand.

Nothing, I tell him, I'm not Christian.

What then, he asks, an edge in his voice, *are you Buddhist?*
    Muslim?

                And then,

I only want to save you from eternal damnation.

                    Denomination.
                    Domination
            To name and to classify.
            To know by looking,
            and through naming.

        To walk in the forest
    and say, *arisaema triphyllum,*
                jack-in-the-pulpit,
                    hypericum punctatum,
                        spotted St. John's-wort.

        Or *boletus luridus*
                (poisonous).

        How to see?
    How to speak without naming,
            without letting the name blind us,
                without letting the name speak
                    by itself.

How will people know me if I write,
                    Natasha Saje,
                white,
            American citizen,
                born in *Munich,*
                    Silesian mother,

Slovene father,
Catholics.

But wasn't there a Polish great-great-grandfather

and a Jew
somewhere on my mother's side?

We Americans don't understand it,

defining difference as we do by looking.

You don't look Indian.
You don't look Jewish.
You don't look black.

When we're all the same shade of brown,

when our bodies have ground out their differences

through eons of intermarriage,

when we speak the same language,

when...

Then they look the same as you, the Muslims,

how can you tell what they are if they look the same?

Well, there's always the name.

Mine's a riddle.

In Slovene "saje" means soot.

In villages and cities where carbon
        coats the buildings
            and one's skin
      with the finest layer of black grit—
you get used to it—
        you wipe a finger across your cheek
        and then there's a black
           smudge on your white shirt.

Did they wear dark shirts
    because they couldn't rid themselves
                  of dust?

My mother wouldn't let me be a Girl Scout,
    smacks of Hitler Youth, she said.
        I must have had a German accent once
           because children called me Hitler's Daughter.
  I told them where I was born; I liked
    being different.

My godfather was in Dachau
    where they put straw under his nails
        until it stuck in the pink flesh
        and then they lit it.

One day he was told he'd be killed
    tomorrow
        and the next day
           the Americans liberated the camp.

He's a Catholic priest who's spent
    his life in Germany,
        who won't go back to Slovenia

until every last Communist is dead,
 he says.

    We Americans say, *I'm half Polish and half Italian* or
I'm part Scotch and part Irish.

       In the old country, we buy
souvenirs, trace the headstones of ancestors
    with a reverent finger, feel
              the hills and rivers as part of us.

     What part?

The part longing for a home

                   the part lost

        when people scattered

    from villages and drifted to cities,

          the part that mourns.

Telling who is good from who is bad is not so easy anymore.

On election day a young man hands me a pamphlet:

      Jews are running this country;
      blacks are ruining it.
      Do you want to be turned out
      of your own country?

      From Latin, *contra*, against,

the land lying opposite

or before one.

We are each other's country,

we are each other's marrow:

to be sucked for sustenance,

depleted by disease,

or to grow

richer

and redder

and darker.

The Quiet Americans

for To Nhuan Vy

We hold our glasses out,
then drink.
Two years since the American soldier returned,
told how he'd turned his Claymores
facing up that night: so the warning,
"This side to the enemy,"
pointed to the sky.
His one small act of protest in the war.

He never knew at midnight, a troop of artists
had passed along the dike, suspected,
one day, one of them would sit beside him
listening as he told the story,
suddenly remember stumbling
on the mines
aimed strangely at the heavens.

There were photos and embraces.
But two years now and not a letter
from the soldier.
He can't understand it. I nod
"How could a man who did such a thing forget?"
We turn back to the young singers,
the sad and lovely music.

The Battle Hymn of the Republic

Defending you, my country, hurts
My eyes. I see the drums, the glory,
The marching through the gory,
Unthinkable mud of soldiers' guts

And opened hearts: I want to serve.
I join the military,
Somehow knowing that I'll never marry.
The barracks' silence as I shave

Is secretive and full of cocks.
I think to myself, *What if I'm a queer,*
What if too many years
Go by and then my brain unlocks—

The days seem uniformed,
Crisp salutes in all the trees;
A sandstorm buries the casualties
Of a war. *What if I were born*

This way, I think to myself,
What if I were dead,
An enemy bullet in my head.
I see the oil burning in the Gulf,

Which hurts my eyes. My sergeant cries.
Now he's a real man—
I sucked his cock behind a van
In the Presidio, beneath a sky

So full of orange clouds
I thought I was in love.
I think to myself, *What have
I become?* I lose myself in the crowds

Of the Castro, the months go by
And suddenly they want to lift the ban.
I don't think they can.
I still want to die

My death of honor, I want to die
Defending values I don't understand;
The men I see walking hand in hand
Bring this love song to my mind.

Like This

The storm breaks leaving the limbs far away from being
what happened, the world, like this. Wind still refuses
to choose between the plumes of grasses and the roofs

of the big houses. The agony of nails prying loose.
The swing unhinged. The fleshy roots of an ash exposed
like the paintings of Death embracing a young woman,

that grotesque ecstasy, the looking on a taboo
that's forbidden in memory but permitted in song.
It's up to you to put *a strip of pavement over the abyss*

or for the physicists, the character-mongers,
the self-silenced, the less massive geniuses
to make something of this transparency.

Light, light, the flame is the convention
of the candle the moth circles—its song, its inborn storm.
Is it animal or angel or human to be

on fire? Now space where before we had plantings.
A rip, the atom shower of Monday and Tuesday,
then a difference in the way people look and what they don't say,

kissed as they are on the mouth by the skeleton
of the normal—the reasonable and anxious—man
who lacks only the organs and a tongue.

The light's a long, steady beam, far from being
paradise but far from being only *like this.*
The wires are down, the field itself electrified.

When Mexicans Die
They Build Houses to God

for Norma

Crowded cemeteries
Everyone builds high into the sky
trying to get closer to Jesus
Empty wine bottles
The church bells ringing calling
todo el mundo
to the evening rosary
Poverty as revealed through the use of
flowers and bright colors
like a Mexican's house
yellow red pink blue scarlet purple
You never seen as colorful a cemetery
as a Mexican cemetery.
The lone grave caught between two
towering gravestone *capillas*
without a tombstone to claim its dead
an oblong mound of dirt surrounded
by rusted coffee cans—
plants and stark red geraniums
sprouting from the mound
Proof that flowers, beautiful flowers
really can grow from your chest
from out of your soul
from your mouth and from your heart
if you're a poor Mexican.

Not Quite Peru

Exiled from yourself, you fuse with everything you meet. You
imitate whatever comes close. You become whatever touches you.
—Luce Irigaray, *This Sex Which Is Not One*

At night I sleep without movement in the suburbs of a Phoenix desert, having dreams of hot plants in the Andes, dreams
filled with parents as they talk to me through moldy Peruvian
phone lines from Lima. I dream of their typed letters on fine
onion skin paper, filed, unopened because I don't want to hear or
read about them telling me they know God. When it's closer to
morning and the Arizona desert is already getting hot, I dream of
Peruvian boot prints in short grass, and of wet apples covered in
chocolate that reflect the Aymara faces and the Aymara bodies
who stand in weeds before the picking season begins. And if I've
run too far the day before, trying to lean out, I sometimes dream
of white women's bodies that don't look like bodies, that are
steely and like machines. My mother, with her white skin and
white clothes, will occasionally call from a Peruvian village she is
visiting to tell me none of these things are in the South America
she knows.

"It's just windy," she says. "It makes people shoot guns."

"I keep dreaming of chocolate-covered apples. I dream of
machines," I say.

"We live here. Your father and I should know. Chocolate and
industry are American things."

My mother calls me Terry and so do all her relatives, but I tell
them it's Teresa now.

"I'm taking Spanish classes," I tell my parents, long distance to
Peru. *"Hola,"* I say for thirty dollars. I imagine my mother,
dressed in white, sits on velvet chairs when we talk, that her voice
echoes over polished marble floors.

"You're always Terry, no matter what," my mother says.

Sometimes I try to speak to her in Spanish, tell her I want to live in downtown Phoenix and buy tortillas cheap and hot from the *tortilleria*. I tell her I want to sell on street corners things I can make myself, with my fingers, with these calloused hands I use to lift weights and turn myself into something not quite human. I try not to tell my mother about my body, though. I try not to tell her that every day I lift so many barbells, do so many squats, my clothes fit tighter and men stare. I try not to tell her that I sit in my Spanish classes, trying to become foreign, wanting to pack a gun in a leather shoulder holster and walk stiffly past those barrio boys who take the same classes to laugh at the stilted language their parents speak. I try not to tell my mother that I want to walk past these same boys on the street, sneering and flexing myself at them until they faint. I don't say anything to her about the scar I now have on my stomach from a short knife fight in a fake cantina. I don't tell my parents about the barrio boy I look for every day, the barrio boy who held his gun so close to my face when I was alone once, lifting heavy objects in an old weight room downtown close to where I work.

These things happen to women with muscles, I told myself then, and I keep saying it. So when my parents call, there is little I can say.

"My biceps are bigger," I tell them, touching the scar on my stomach. Lately, muscles are the safest things I can tell my parents about, though I try to play it down. "I win things by flexing in public. I'll send you a picture."

"I hope you win money," my mother says. "What's the point if it doesn't give you something to invest?"

"It'll keep her out of trouble," my father says from another line.

"Have money so you won't need it," my mother says. "And remember, white people don't have to sell tortillas."

Their financial advice is good, but the rest I try to ignore. I lie outside in the sun and inside in tanning booths until my white skin doesn't look white. I eat tortillas before and after my heavier workouts, sitting in the sauna with a rag full of corn ones, chewing their dry, yellow textures. I sweat and think of yellow, the yellow of the barrio boy's shirt, the way the color reflected off his gun, the way his teeth reflected everything.

I try to think of other things, like the way the color yellow looks so very deep and bright on the school bus I see every morning on my way to the bank, the bus full of children screaming, my bank boss's children waving at me, making muscles at me through the thick windows that keep them all from jumping. When men in Jeeps and suits stare at me as we drive to the downtown where we all work, I kiss my rolled-up window and leave lipstick stains there to make them think twice. And as I drive into the basement of the bank, I stare back at the staring Latinos waiting for the morning grapefruit trucks.

"If you eat too many tortillas, soon you'll be speaking nothing but Spanish," my mother says during another long-distance conversation where bad connections require us to repeat everything we say.

"You should know about Spanish and tortillas," I tell her.

"Spanish is good," my father says. "I speak it. I eat tortillas. I was born in Juarez, you know." Each time I call, my father tells the story of his father's goats being buried by sand in the Sonoran desert. And I always laugh, long distance.

"Goats move too much," my mother says. "Anyway, if your daughter came down here, I bet she'd be shooting guns with the rest of them. I bet she'd be one of those communists."

"They're Maoists," I say. I try to think of the word for "bourgeois" in Spanish, but nothing comes. My Spanish book doesn't list it, and only has words like "dog," "rain," "apartment," "rent." Because I don't think the Maoists would care much for my textbook Spanish, I tell my mother I could never visit them there in that place where people shoot and touch you too much, where people get too close to you with guns.

"Moving around isn't for me," I tell my parents. "I have to stay where it's warm and people understand what I'm talking about."

"Of course you can move. People are the same everywhere," my mother says. My father hums on the other line, reading.

Sometimes, I can't move from the dusty chair I'm sitting in right now, I want to tell them, but I don't. Sometimes all I can do is sit here, and if it is spring, I will watch desert tornados start to swirl. And when the dust in the sky turns yellow, like the yellow of his shirt so close to my face, I do push-ups, I do sit-ups, I grab the bar in the kitchen doorway and pull until my head is too full and

I almost want to kill like Maoists who shoot with quiet faces.

These parents of mine, they move and talk so much their motions upset the balance of things. At least that's what Linda tells me, Linda, my trainer who once lifted herself, who says she is partly Navajo. Linda whose blond, muscular words make my body something other. And I do believe everything she says with her promises of bulk, cuts, and trophies. I do believe her as she gives me half-kisses between the strain of powerlifting sets, when I'm pushing at weight until my skin is about to rip open.

This is what I try to think of when I remember the boy in yellow.

"Balance is all there is," Linda says one day, using her pinky to pull slightly at the middle of the bench-press bar I'm straining with in the middle of this weight room, a room I sometimes have dreams about at night as my large muscles twitch. When we first started here, when I had a body no one noticed, a body without veins, when Linda was still competing, and pushing her muscles at thin-haired judges, that was when the men who lift here used to ignore us. But now they stare as I strain, as my arms get bigger than theirs, as the muscle striations I pull at daily start to make me look like the metal I lift.

"You must have everything in alignment," Linda says as we sit in her suburban home, as she massages me, and then, as she carefully folds my socks, placing them in a circle around me as I sit on the bed waiting for her to use the spiritual Navajo phrases that will help me win trophies and money and fear with my body.

This is how Linda and I spend our nights, concentrating on the things that prepare us and our muscles for competition. We used to watch television when I first moved in. I was thin and unspectacular and never wanted to speak Spanish. Linda even used to kiss me, uncertain about what or who to love. Now she is more certain and kisses no one. Now I am told to sit on the bed and breathe in powerful words as she surrounds me with socks or with food, anything that is round, and thus, more spiritual. This almost Navajo woman turns out lights and makes me watch the ritual candle she holds, the blue flame of it, the way it moves back and forth when we breathe. It will, she says, make me forget the judges who grope and stare during competitions. When asphalt is melting outside on Phoenix streets, and Linda is saying her Navajo power words over me, the words that will make the judges know I am perfect, I always feel a small sweat moving over my shoulders as if I was coming down from a sugar binge.

But this is not the time for a binge, Linda tells me. We have to be flexing and hard in the morning. We have to be completely without fat or sweat.

"We have to be mechanical," she likes to say, and I like to hear it. Machine words make me feel like small, perfect molecules. Some nights she'll even say I'm "Steely" as she reads aloud from her Navajo books, trying to better learn the language she thinks her father spoke.

"We do not eat chocolate or fatty foods," she says in English, and then in Navajo. She tries to translate everything she says into this Indian language, sometimes making me repeat after her as I strain my deltoids with dumbbells. She is always saying words I will never know or be able to pronounce.

But this is how a bodybuilder gains spirituality, and we are bodybuilder people, she tells me. She makes me watch myself flex in the bedroom mirror every night before we go to bed, celibate and tingling with the spent cells of muscle and incense and Navajo incantations.

"There are lots of jobs I have to do here," I tell my parents when they ask me, again, to visit them in their Andean jungle, to tour the mountains of cocaine and poppy fields with them during the spring mists. "I lift weights, you know. My possessions are here. My car, my mascara, my Spanish class, my pets." Of course, I have no pets, but mothers like them. Pets, like muscles, make them feel like their daughters will live through anything.

"You shouldn't have too many things. You're still young," they say, sounding almost like the Maoists they despise. They themselves are in denial, always saying "no" to things, "no" to materiality, "no" to new paint for their flaking walls I see in the pictures they send. They say "no" to new shoes, they tell me, and put their Mercedes up on blocks, refusing to drive it anywhere out of a fear of God and things manmade.

"When you're dead, objects won't matter," my mother says. "We can't take our Mercedes with us. So why should we drive it now?"

"You should buy something, paint the house, live in a condo," I tell them, but they don't listen. Their walls keep flaking. Their pool gets holes in the plaster as the water evaporates, unused. Their grass gets diseases.

"We're just like monks," they say.

"Monks are good," Linda tells me later. "They know what they need and they know how to get it."

These spare parental conversations from Peru make me dream at night of the Latin women my mother talks about, the ones I want to be like. Or I dream of a Linda who kisses my lips with real kisses. Of course, I don't tell my parents any of this. And I don't tell Linda. She always makes symbols out of things. If I dream of Oreos, she says it means there is a black woman named Carla whose muscles I will beat someday soon in competition.

"We are in training so everything is meaningful," Linda would say. "The sand we run on swirls to make patterns that tell us things. The air particles tell us how close we are to becoming bigger."

"Some people don't want to be big," I tell her. "Some people want to go unnoticed, be blank and invisible."

"Only the holy can be invisible," she says.

At the bank where I work, I speak in numbers. My boss looks hard at me when the loan season is slow, when men aren't borrowing money to finance a boat or a mistress or a desert pool. My boss looks hard at me and I can tell he is one of those who thinks I am too big.

"That suit, it doesn't look right on you," he says. And it's true. I look at myself in the building windows at lunch, my rippling reflection walking past mirrored glass, my well-defined calf muscles pushing at panty hose I will soon stop wearing. My legs are men's legs. Drag queens who walk downtown, pretending their husbands have sent them out to shop, stop and ask me for advice as I eat enchiladas outside by noisy pigeons. I invite them to sit and have lunch, and this is how I end up in cafés eating lunch with those who are more beautiful than me, their transvestite faces more perfect than the gloss of magazine faces, their waists thin and ready for photographs. We talk about makeup and posture, and I nod at their questions as the outside heat saps me of what little moisture Linda has allowed me to have. When these men walk with me back to the bank, the barrio boys whistle at all of us.

Once, I sent my now Peruvian parents a picture, me in a posing bikini, my body oiled, my G-string tight, my gluteals twice the size they were when my parents last saw me three years ago. They called to say I looked nice.

"Things sure change," my father said.

"Yes," my mother said. "In my day even the men were flabby."

"I was skinny like a fence," my father said.

"My father was big, but he didn't have muscle," my mother said. "His voice was very muscular, though."

"It sure is nice to talk to you," my father said.

"Is that oil on you?" my mother asked. "You look wet. Is your bikini wet? I didn't even know you wore bikinis."

"I saw a woman like that at the fair once," my father said.

"If we had those kinds of women here, they would live in the hills," my mother said. "They would shoot guns."

Without thinking, I told them what I had been telling them for years about all my activities. "It's normal. Everyone does it."

"If you were here, you would live in the hills. You would shoot guns, too. You just like to fight," my mother said, and for a moment I felt exposed. I touched my stomach scar, the scar I should get removed, Linda tells me, the scar that reminds me of the real anger I saw that night in the cantina I went to looking for the yellow shirt, for the barrio boy and his gun, but only finding an angry man with a knife. He had the kind of anger, the kind of face I so seldom see at my air-conditioned job or at Linda's desert home. He was yelling at the wall when I walked in, seeing the *Cervezas* sign flash from the road, thinking I might like to look around after a long day of bank meetings and numbers.

"*Pendejos,*" he yelled. He was sweating, drinking from a bottle, spinning around to make sure no one was behind him. Everyone else was standing against the wall farthest from the man, drinking or staring. I stood at the door, understanding his intensity, wanting to touch the man, to taste some of his emotion. He looked at me when I did, and then my shirt was split, and there was blood staining my expensive suit as everyone ran out behind us.

And so it is difficult to have this scar removed, even when the judges at bodybuilding events tell me they can't see my abdominals clearly enough with a scar like that in the way. They say it looks like cheating, like I have muscles where I shouldn't.

Because I have scars I don't want my parents to see, because I sometimes believe what my mother says about guns, that I would shoot them if I were there, because of this I tell them I will never visit them, never fly three thousand miles away from the sandy dryness of this Phoenix desert. But sometimes I do imagine living in Peru. Sometimes I imagine coming out of bushes surrounded by mist and rain, wearing green camouflage, wearing large earrings and someone else's muddy boots that don't fit. I would be a *guerrilla* with muscles, and go to villages to tell people they must stop buying food with English or Japanese writing on the labels. I will tell them that potatoes are better, more natural, more Peruvian, and less capitalistic. But when I dream of this, they all say they're bored with potatoes. They say they hate imported beans.

"We aren't Peruvians, either," they say in my dreams.

While I'm awake, after workouts, I sit in locker room saunas, imagining that in South America I would be a woman with a shoulder-slung AK-47. I would have to keep pushing it out of the way as I tell these villagers how to cook different potato dishes through frying and basting and breadifying. But these Aymaras don't listen. They draw pictures of cars and curvy women in the dark Peruvian mud and look at each other. Sometimes I imagine flexing for them when I help lift boxes full of market vegetables ready to sell for guns. When I'm flexing they touch my white, muscled skin with their fingernails. I want to name my muscles for them, say "deltoid" and "latissimus," but those words don't come to me without dictionaries.

These people call me transparent in my dreams.

"You look like coca leaves," they tell me. I smile because they say that is the highest compliment to give a white person in Peru, even if I am really a mestizo.

Sometimes as I lie on the carpeted weight room floor, the one that is safe from guns and full of white men who want to do things to me but never will, that is when I think of Peru. I like to imagine letting the Indian women there put lipstick on my lips and arms so they can see it stain.

"You are like rocks at low elevations," they say. "Large and smooth." They seem to like this drawing time we share. They smile as their lipstick leaves marks like dark berries on my skin.

"You've got to get that out of your mind," Linda says, rubbing my scar, trying to make it fade before the judges complain. "Peru is no place for a woman with muscles."

I am sitting on an old examination bed in the auditorium hallway before my first competition, before my first time flexing in bikini, in oil, in public. This will be the picture I send my parents later, the one they will think is nice, the one where I'm oiled in bikini, on a bed with a hand over my scar as if I were laughing so hard I had to hold my stomach in. I tell Linda to take the picture. This way my parents will never see her face that is so thin and ravaged by the life and cigarettes they would call evil.

Men in dark suits walk by as Linda takes pictures of me and my muscles so my parents can see what I am doing to myself. She puts oil on my lats as men ask me questions about my bodybuilding past, how long I've competed, how much I weigh, what my biceps' circumference is.

"You are a big one," these men tell me, making me get on a scale. It says one hundred forty-two, the most I have weighed without fat.

"She has to concentrate," Linda says, moving in front of them, snapping her fingers at me to help me focus.

In the bathroom she opens a makeup kit for me and we start to put powders and colors on my face, bits at a time. She puts eyeliner in my hand, but all I do is hold it.

"A little charcoal would look good here," she says, pointing at my eyelid.

"A little charcoal," I say. I am dazed, staring and hot from a lack of food, not sweating from a lack of water, nervous about showing my body off in front of yelling crowds, in front of suited men.

My fingers are twitching with shaky nerves and a low supply of electrolytes. This is normal, everyone says, and everyone does it, they all say, so there must be some kind of safety.

"You can't afford to bloat," they say.

I have learned that safety is not a word for them. Food and bloated stomachs and saturated skin cells are foreign, evil things. I think of bloating, my skin swelling a little, my muscle cuts fading into a mush like Darryl's body, the man I once almost loved, especially for his cooking. My stomach growls as I think of his recipes, so I think of the Andes instead, of bodies bloating in bushes, of their muscles fading, too, but for different reasons. These would be the ones who got too close to people with guns on a windy day, my mother might tell me. Maybe if it were windy here, I, too, would want to get a gun out, a gun I will maybe buy later, or take from a barrio boy. I think of him again, the boy in yellow, even though I know Linda would not approve if she knew. I think of the way he touched my arm, pushed his fingernails into the muscle, leaving red marks.

"You think you're big," he said. I lay there on a dusty bench, still holding the barbell above in its metal support arms, feeling the pressure of veins in my neck as I became speechless and angry. "If you were a woman, I'd fuck you." He laughed, then looked at the door as if someone he had been running from might come in, blasting.

And if there is a day when I go by a gun store downtown, I might get the same kind of gun he had, and if I take it out, I may try to blow away some sneering boy in yellow who thinks he can touch me and laugh. I would leave this kind of boy in the weeds close to a baseball field, later to be found by children.

But in Phoenix, the winds are hot and slow, and seldom do white women like me shoot hot bullets.

"Your eyes are slightly dilated. Make a fist for a few minutes," Linda tells me now, her voice so quiet. I can feel heat rising in my neck. All colors and objects at this cheap bodybuilding contest seem far away. I'm beginning not to care what my face looks like or what kind of color Linda is putting on me.

"I don't care," I tell Linda. "Everything is fuzzy." I look at her, and her eyes are dark blue but speaking foreign languages. Navajo, she says. But still, she is American, she is blond and does her laundry at home while watching the news, while wishing for the cigarettes she gave up years ago. When she sits in the kitchen, wanting to smoke, her mouth says unspiritual things about sex and hate no matter how much she burns sage and reads her Navajo books, telling me she wants to live in Sedona Arizona and become holy like her Navajo relatives.

"That's why we can't kiss," she tells me at night. "You and I need to be empty and clean. We need to be invisible." She sits on the carpet and, instead of smoking, paints her nails in un-Navajo fruit colors as I fall asleep on her bed and feel my large quads twitching.

"Close your eyes," she tells me now in the auditorium bathroom that smells of sweaty competition and chlorine. These are the smells of powders and perfume that muscular women use to make their faces look less like machines. In front of me, in Linda's hand, there is that sharp point of a pencil eyeliner that drags my skin into clumps when I do it myself. But Linda's fingers are cool as they hold my chin. She spritzes my forehead and puts on the sweet-smelling base. Light rouge is brushed on quickly, the brush pricking my cheeks. Then the sparkling powder she says the judges will like in those lights is blown on to hold it all in.

"That's not me," I say at the mirror. My face has changed. It looks like the face I see on so many other women as they try to do what their bosses tell them.

"That's much more you," my mother says when she sees the close-up photo, me in makeup and an almost real hairdo with small curls. I would not go to a barrio with this kind of makeup. I would not pack a gun with this hair.

"You are so pretty," my parents say. But no one ever calls me pretty. And I don't want them to. My muscles get in the way, and when I flex them, I think of flaky pastries and Irish Cream, things I cannot eat. I think of Peruvian villagers touching me with charcoal fingers. I think of clenching my buttocks for the judges. I don't think of being pretty.

Now, onstage for the first time, I unprettily flex for the first time in front of a large audience, and the dizziness of bright lights and cigarette smoke make me want to just stop moving and fall onto the stage floor in front of the judges. But I know Linda is out there looking at me, saying magical words for me, so I avoid falling by not moving my feet or doing any twisting or turning. I flex in place, and still, I get applause.

When I work, I am corporate, letting my barbell-calloused hands finesse bank statements, allowing my muscular lips to tell people if they can have ten thousand dollars or not. At work, I wield the power of finance, and I feel guilt because of it.

"You are so bourgeois," Linda says, though she herself wields power with the governor of our Arizona. She is his supreme executive secretary. She helps him understand that the blueprints he makes have an effect on his spirituality. She points out that the way he walks and thinks can put holes where they weren't meant to be in a desert that doesn't want them.

"But you wear two-hundred-dollar suits," I tell Linda, trying to find inconsistencies in a woman who lives for contradiction.

"My suits are natural. Yours are not," she says.

This is sometimes the only thing we talk about anymore when weights aren't being pulled or magical Navajo words aren't being invoked or I'm not watching yellow desert storms.

Still, I do feel sorry when I'm in my expensive and unnatural power suits, sitting over oak desks with clients. Last month I tried to buy some suits in a donation center, but the woman at the cash register looked at me too much. She saw my clean, tanned white skin, my impractical leather shoes, my too finely combed hair, all in somebody else's unwanted, crumpled suit. She knew I was a fraud.

At work, I've been nothing but problems with my occasional discount suits and bulging body.

"No one has thighs like that," my boss says. He calls me in a lot now. Lately I've had trouble saying no to men in cowboy hats and large belt buckles who want ten thousand dollars to start iguana purse factories in Peoria. I want to tell my boss that money doesn't mean that much, that people should be able to buy any kind of purse they want, and that I should be able to let them.

"I think people like unique accessories," I tell my boss.

"This isn't California." He always breathes a lot when I'm in his office, wanting to ask me to flex for him, I know, but he doesn't ask. When I leave, he watches my calf muscles as I walk.

Though I have been at the bank for years, now that I am big, the cameras there follow me more often as I walk clients to the outer offices, or take copy jobs to the secretaries, or stop to stare at the women in yellow shirts. As I walk up and down with spreadsheets and financial profiles, these cameras quietly spin in any direction on high-tech hydraulics, zooming in on parts of my legs, I'm sure, or my thick neck with the turn of a lens. Linda tells me it's just jealousy, that people have always wanted to look at what they can't have.

"Even I still get stares," she tells me, almost flexing her thin arm. "A body like this can hypnotize."

"I don't think it's jealousy," I tell her. I always look behind me now when I walk around the office, trying not to turn as I imagine the hum of cameras coming into focus.

In the early evenings when Linda is working late at the capitol, telling the governor how to behave, I watch as the sun bleaches the yards in our neighborhood, turns all the cactus gardens full of painted rocks white, and all the lawns light yellow. Linda's house is too close to the desert for such civilized things to survive. Dust and jackrabbits eat away at any hints of excess or careful pruning. Javelinas with their wild pig snouts and black hair lie dead and bloating on the eighteenth hole of nearby executive golf courses, unaware of the havoc their smelling bodies cause.

I clean my short, practical nails while the dust storms of late summer hit, burying newly planted sod, blowing quartz crystals from rock gardens into the road, bending the tall yuccas people have brought in from our backyard desert to see if they would grow next to roses and purple snapdragons. Our neighbors pat manure around the base of their yuccas, but still their hollow stocks bend, still their pods blow down the street past station wagons trying to get in out of the dust and swirling desert bushes.

When it's dark and the monsoon lightning storms are flashing by South Mountain, I read makeup magazines to improve my skills for Linda and the judges, or at least that is what I tell Linda.

Lately, I've become more interested in the bras than the eyeliners or lipsticks. There is always a lure to a piece of clothing you haven't worn for years, the containment of it unneeded for so long. I look at the advertising photos, trying to remember if I ever had breasts like that, and what it might have felt like to hold them, to even be able to lift them up or see them sway. Linda made my breasts disappear long ago with all her reps and diets. Now these magazine bras and women's bodies seem so foreign, they pull my eyes in. Sometimes, when the models all look pillowy and full of curves, I have to cut out pictures of them in their Maidenforms and Balis, put them in a file I keep at the office so Linda won't see. She would say they were a distraction.

"Women's bodies will break you," she would say.

When it's lunchtime and the office is eating in, licking fallen mayonnaise off their desks while clients wait outside, I look at my bra pictures, and at these bra models without stomach muscles. Their mammaries would shock the bodybuilding world. I touch the glossy pages where the bras are highlighted. I tabulate interest rates for my next client, and think of calling the phone number at the bottom of one bra ad, a 1-800 number for sharing bra mishaps and complaints about fit and color and unnatural rashes, problems I haven't had for years.

There are days when I watch my clients waiting, sitting, and cleaning their own nails as they hope they've told me the right things to receive the big loans. I watch the camera in front of my office as it zooms in on them and their fidgeting, their crossing legs, their constant physical readjustments. As the camera in the outer office focuses on me through my executive window, I tabulate figures more rapidly, and think of phoning that number, of calling up the bra receptionists who no doubt have big breasts, who I'm sure wear nothing but a bra when they talk to their callers so assuredly.

One day, after a night of dreaming, a night full of starvation dreams and yellow-shirted Hispanic men, I do call, right there after lunch, my boss walking by my door every so often to try and look at my leg muscles hidden by desk. I listen to the computerized messaging service and push buttons until a real person talks.

"Service Center," a woman says.

"I have a lot of questions. Do I just start asking them?" I look up and wave first at my client, then at my boss.

"That's what we're here for."

"Do you know about underwires? Mine doesn't fit very well." I try to remember a conversation I had with my favorite transvestite last week, and I try to talk like him. The camera lens above my secretary moves slightly, so I cover the ad on my desk with my hand, turn in my swivel chair to face the outside window.

I try to imagine what this phone woman looks like as I listen to her explain the variations I could try to get my breasts to cooperate, if only I had them. I want to ask her what her body looks like, if it is like the model on the page in my hand. I want to tell her I lied, that I don't have the kind of body that requires the extra support of bras, but I don't say anything about this.

"Do you enjoy talking to women?" I ask her.

"I like my job very much," she says.

At night when Linda's house moves in slow motion around my starving and breastless body, and when Linda is working late with the governor, and when all I can think about is the food she won't let me have, and the way that her deprivations and the barrio boy's violence make me feel so weak and small, I start to make phone calls I don't tell anyone about.

"Have you ever tried a Maidenform Bra?" I ask women I have picked from the phone book, drinking soda water after soda water that Linda has told me will make me bloat. No doubt tomorrow she will see it, the bloating, the soda water coming out of my pores, the empty bottles covered over in the kitchen trash can. This is all I can do when Linda won't let me binge, when she tells me bloating would be like death for someone with a body like mine.

But there are times when being reckless is all that keeps me from lying on the couch for days without moving just to feel the slow atrophy of muscle, and the invisibility of being still.

When I talk about bras to these phone book women, I drink mineral waters with abandon, using my best corporate voice to make them talk.

"We are doing a bra survey this evening," I say, sipping.

"Are you selling them?" the women on the phone ask. When I

tell them I'm not selling, they always want to buy, they always want to ask me the questions I wanted to ask the woman with the hotline service.

"What stores do you usually buy your brassieres in, madam?" I try to remember the days when I would walk into a store and try bras on, the saleswoman bringing me different sizes and colors, asking me if she could come in to see how they fit.

"Bra stores?" says the woman on the phone. "Frank will only buy me red ones, but they stain my skin." I look at the front door to make sure Linda isn't opening it as I ask for more details, as I pry into another woman's life. Sometimes I can keep them on the phone for half an hour as I tease them with a potential sale or a new bra that would drive any man or woman crazy. This is all I can think to do some nights when it's too hot for kissing or knife fights, and my body seems so big and unnecessary, so fearful of movement, so holy it starts to disappear beneath me.

After a workout of fast moving squats, and slow pull-downs needed to emphasize my obliques, I walk slowly up weight room stairs to the gray company car I will drive to Linda's desert house, my muscles acid-filled and heavy. As I walk, I think of Darryl, my lovely, fat ex, and his cooking, his sticky sweet kisses many months away now, but living only a few blocks down from Linda's.

"Darryl will make you bloat," Linda tells me, afraid her former bodybuilding partner will do to me what he did to her, make me bloat, make me want to lie on couches for days and smoke.

"Linda will starve you," Darryl says. "She'll sap your muscles right out from under you." He is always chewing on the phone. His cooking noises make my holy and deprived stomach squirm.

"Darryl will kill you," Linda says. "Darryl has killed many things." She always goes into the kitchen when she speaks about him. She talks about his bloated body while holding imaginary cigarettes between her fingers. Sometimes I see Darryl outside on his sandy desert lawn, walking around his house in flowered shirts, his legs strangely white. These legs of his make me want to talk to him, smell the richness of his cooking, binge once again with him until we are in comas.

"I'm thinner now," I tell Darryl on the phone, secretly, hiding in the bathroom while Linda makes lettuce sandwiches.

"I could make you the most incredible chocolate cheesecake," he says. "Syrup dripping off the top."

"God," I say.

Linda knocks on the door.

"I can see the cord," she says. "Tell Darryl to fuck off."

"Fuck off, honey," I tell my old boyfriend who wants to make me fat so I will stay with him.

"That wasn't a very holy thing to say," I tell Linda later after I've hung up. I walk into the kitchen and pinch at my very thin skin for her, slap at my heavy quads for her to see my transparent leanness. "He says I'm too thin."

"That's the idea," Linda says. "Lean and nothing but sinew and fiber. That's the only way to win." She touches my cheek with a fingernail, pinches at my gluteals, but there is nothing to pinch when I'm flexing.

At night when Linda is painting her nails or learning new Navajo words, I sometimes think of Darryl kissing me in the desert like he once used to, the one-hundred-ten-degree sand sticking to our legs as snakes watched from under bushes. That is sometimes what I think of as I fall asleep with celibate but muscular lips, trying to feel the imaginary sand between my fingers, the kiss of Darryl's sweetness, and as I dream of Darryl instead of the color yellow, Linda and her nail-polish smells fade.

In the afternoons after a day of banking and bra phone calls, after yelling *"pendejo"* at every barrio boy I see from the safety of my car, I like to run through the tall saguaros and junipers in the desert behind Linda's house, the desert Darryl once kissed me in, sand and dead lizards hitting the backs of my calves like they used to hit the backs of Darryl's calves when he would run, when his body was as hard as mine. I like the way sand sticks to my shoulders and hair, and I do sprints as snakes sidewind patterns on the trail in front of me. This is where children play behind our neighborhood houses, hide behind prickly pears, throw dead yuccas at each other, and watch the skin of their hands melt on anything they touch.

This is the place I watch these children from as I run on a circular path, the one all the husbands and ex-husbands run on in the mornings when the snakes have receded. They tell me their running makes them more aggressive at work. But for me, it is a way of celebrating, of knowing I am more powerful than others. My boss himself lives down the street by Darryl, and he runs here in the mornings, but his eyes make me nervous. His children watch Linda and me in the kitchen as we almost kiss over tabouli salads on the weekends, Linda always pulling away and smiling.

Still, my boss knows I'm a banker who can kill with a look, who can bleed loan payments out of clients with a word on the fax that makes their secretaries feel fear. And so he hesitates to fire me. What he doesn't know is that I'm a loan officer almost packing a .44 I will buy to shoot at things when the heat is pushing in on me, when the winds are blowing in Peru, when my body is even more of a foreign thing my parents will not have any words for.

Maybe when I have a gun, and I have sat polishing its blueness for hours, and felt the movement of its parts, maybe then I will even shoot at people in South Phoenix during the sandy season if Linda and her constant flow of words and starvation tactics keep pushing my adrenaline to new highs. Maybe if I can't stop thinking of that sneering barrio boy in the empty weight room, of being alone with him, his gun in my face, my large muscles immobilized, unmoving, useless, if I can't stop thinking of the yellowness of that, maybe then shooting will be the only release.

"I kill with a flex," I say before every competition, and in every mirror, trying to believe it. "My muscles can flatten you," I say before every loan appraisal. "My hands are dangerous," I say as I drive by cantinas in South Phoenix, wishing it were true.

Tribe

Half of us were enrolled in the Army.
Half of us were not. Half of us
watched for thieves in the factories
and were given no sleep. Half
recited the day's events into machines
equipped with sensitive needles.
Half never stopped training, and buried
dried food at spots marked in red
on maps. The songs half of us
sang were designed to confuse.
We exchanged flags regularly. Half
of us marched in weekly parades and
threw stones at foreign-owned shops.
We were beaten in jail. Our wounds were
photographed. Half of us pled assigned pleas
before hostile tribunals. Some of us
wore blindfolds at night and were pushed
into fields of damp soy. Some had diseases
of the blood. Half of us carried
bricks of hashish across the Eastern boundary
in the heels of our shredded boots.
Half attended the annual party of the
ruling elite. Some of us had sex.
Half of us worked at the paper or radio
or as clerks in the offices of government
bookkeepers. All returned home by circuitous
routes. Half of us studied an ancient dialect
which was used as a code. Half painted abstract
slogans on discarded bedsheets. A few
could be found lighting candles at the apse
of the damaged Cathedral. A few carried
chains in their purses. Some played cricket

and one was a baritone in the Men's Choir.
Two or three walked on as spear holders
at the Palais de l'Opéra. None of us joked
about the heavy briefcases some of us kept.
Half of us endured ritual purges. Half bathed
in hot oils. Half had their skin color
altered. Half were removed from circulation
without notice and reappeared later
at exotic locales. Not all reappeared.
Some were in therapy. Some sold fabricated
memoirs to the State. Many were buried in caves.
Half of us pursued the enemy at all costs
into the jagged streets, avoiding the traps
laid by sympathizers. Half of us
are unknown to the rest of us.
Half of us will be arriving tomorrow by boat.
Half of us are here.

Spring

That morning—a humid morning, early Spring, gray birds
feeding on muddy lawns, the sound of a chain saw
nearby, a red shirt tied to a battered tree,
the empty smoke-streaked sky—

That morning they held him in the green car
and negotiated his punishment. They blindfolded him.
His hand was held to something very hot and then to something
very cold. He was told to pray and he did.
Then he was hit. Then he thought he smelled a woman.
He was asked how he liked it.

They could make it look like an accident.
They could litter the scene with mysterious clues.
There were many such examples of their expertise
on the public record. But he didn't care what had happened
in the past

to others. He tried to remember the end of a story
that he had been told as a child by a woman
with a high-pitched voice. It was a story much like
this one. Its moral was the love of God.
He was confused. He was brought back by salts.
Now two stories crossed in his mind

and were hard to distinguish.
The heroes of both stories could not be trusted.
In the green car he felt he liked both stories.
He couldn't decide.
They removed the blindfold and put drops in his eyes

that made him see in black and white.
He loved the Spring. The idea of being
punished in the Spring was easier for him.

Good reasons could be given.
It could be said that he defaced the ancient city walls.
It could be said that he burned public goods
and stood in the frightened crowd, watching.
It could be said that he had touched the children
offensively. All of this could be said

and there was more. Now it was raining.
He stood at the fairgrounds
with its rows of empty concrete benches.
All around him birds were feeding on earthworms.
It didn't feel like punishment.
It felt wet. A hole opened in the ground
and he fell into it.

Help

You took the room in the attic. Watched
television by yourself. I used to walk
down the dim stairs to the basement to be
with you at night, to listen to stories
of plantations and dictatorships as you
folded with precise care the underpants
of my family. You who knew our human stains:
faint arrowheads of feces and blood.

Often at suppertime
an ungovernable sadness came over me
as you ate by yourself in the kitchen,
after moving around the mahogany table
with bowls of string beans and tin-wrapped
baked potatoes. I never understood why
you could not sit with us when every morning
you tied my shoes, buttered my toast,
placed an extra Oreo in my lunch box.

After I left, it was you
who held my mother every afternoon as she watched
her mother consumed by the hidden black grapes
of malignancy, embracing beside the kitchen sink
while *Days of Our Lives* flickered in the background.
Still, she insisted on disguising you in uniforms
of pink and white. And I believe it had to do
with your skin: black as ebony, and your palms—
lighter, the color of milk chocolate.

Shining hands entering
my restless bedroom at night, with a washcloth
that was cool, and a spoon dripping honey.

Labor Day

In a coffee can his flower
beside loose bricks
ledged on a city rowhouse
gerrymandered for six kids,
roosts of rooms, tilting floors,
swayback roof sloping
toward a Baltimore shipyard
still as a world war watch

Iggy Jones, old boilermaker,
the belly on him,
down to two cigars a day,
living off the mailman's pouch
and luncheonette shank stew,
fries sunken in the gravy,
but hungry for the past

leans into the morning
from the brown of a room,
tips a jug over the flower
pouring as if it was milk
into six kitchen mugs,
then hangs his stars and stripes
held to the ledge with bricks
from the shipyard.

Cousins

High. Mindless. Cackle at the edge of the world.
And the geese are flying there

and crying, for two weeks now they've come racketing
each morning, miles and miles of them, pouring.

Where do they come from, where did they sleep
last night?

I can't see them, but the question ticks like a clock

about to strike. In the East there are golf courses, soft beds
where they can fatten and die.

But here there are only prairies. Stubbled
hayfields. And a few marshes.

Sluggish, with wet trickles,
snakes twisting where they rest

until they rise again, into cold
scurrying clouds rattling. The mad yammer

and rasp of them is a zipper,
a sewing machine clacking.

As if anyone could interpret

the sounds they make, which are nasal. Long and
narrow.

Something is weaving through the blood

we don't know. Right now, in the bedroom
the radio in my head switches channels: the latest flu virus

from Asia swims across the ocean, head crammed
in the dank holds of barges, in the stuffy cabins

of superjets, microbes riding the tall air
over our heads to Montana where the geese clamor

like hounds baying after ghosts. Like confused hunters
with rifles chattering, doubling back on themselves, where are we

and where are we going? In the East,
nowhere. Stopped dead. On green fairways

nesting all year among golf balls.

In the Midwest the subdivisions multiply
so fast over their feeding places

finally the State of Minnesota heaps them all up

into Boeing 747's heading South, airlifted
over their own flyways.

Now, listening to them babble

out there on the horizon, ribboning along the crack
between earth and sky undulating

like oiled rivers, endless
as the coils of a Greek meander,

what's lost is among us
streaming along the arteries and the bones

of gazelles. Polar bears. Spiders.
Porpoises wallowing in nets, sweet chlorophyll

in autumn leaving the trees, the crisp scarlet molecules
brittle now, and dying, what if they don't

ever come back? Wild, frantic-seeming

as carnival barkers, each year with these families
in their ragged echelons, I can't tell

what they're saying but I feel them

like brothers and sisters, each following the same
or almost the same secret instructions for flying

as I do, cousins calling to each other
to stick together, but even as we cry out

from cold marshes, from estuaries with cells flooding
into grainfields and even golf courses, from the far reaches

of the Arctic tundra, out of the darkness honking

the geese are going now, in the predawn
mists of consciousness they flow over us and beyond.

Foucault in Vermont

No author for this fall landscape, nor signs
Of limits tested, except the fence just yards
From I-89, and a stray Holstein
Unfazed by traffic heading for the border.
How different from your time in California,
Those LSD trips at Zabriskie Point,
Warm nights spent cruising, or in Castro's bars
With studded whips and chains, implements
Not of love but knowledge: "to find God—
Or truth—in moments when the greatest pain
And pleasure are melted into one." De Sade
And de Chardin. The virus swarms your brain...
But now this woolen hat. No melting here,
A state fist-fucked by winter every year.

Outside Magdalena, Sonora

The waiter called me over from my table with a wave. It was a wave first with his hand, but then with his eyebrow and his smile, and with a nod of his head to be sure. He called me over more with these than with his hand, and so I got up. In an unfamiliar place, one pays attention. One uses for ears the eyes as well.

But this attentiveness was not for much. The waiter, who turned out to be the owner, was simply occupied with washing glasses and didn't want to be bothered with coming over to my table. He thought I was the good sort, and that I wouldn't mind, he said. So he had taken the chance, that I would not be offended. And anyway, a person always took a chance one way or another with strangers, didn't I think so?

He looked at me up and down with his bigger eye. He did it in such a manner that I knew I need not answer his question. That eye also said it had not seen me around here before. But if he indeed said anything aloud, his words were muffled behind the plate he was drying by blowing on it. He had done the same with each of the glasses, a shake, a little drying, and then blowing.

The rhythm of it all should have been comforting, but it was not. It said instead that the waiter, the owner, knew what to do, and I did not. I had the menu, but he knew what to do with the glasses.

The place was open-air after entering, a restaurant and a bar and a coffeehouse all in one. Just behind and to the side of him was an opening to a garden, a whole wall missing, but leading to tables surrounded by bougainvillea and ivy.

Without turning to see where I was glancing, he said to me, "It's very beautiful, don't you think? Everyone goes to sit out there. And why not. Except for the bees, and sometimes the wasps, it's perfect. I put up some nets for shade. Do you like them?"

I nodded my head, even though I couldn't see them. I could only see the shade. "It looks very nice," I said. I was a little embarrassed as the words stayed a little too long in my mouth.

I had come here to this town in Sonora from Arizona, and my Spanish was good, but certainly not perfect. It's just what had happened through the years and between generations. But we came from the small towns here, in the middle and in the north of Sonora, Rayón and Cucurpe, San Ignacio, towns like this one. I was in the right place.

"Then that is where you should sit. Come on." He wiped his hands on his apron, got what seemed to be a menu different from what I was holding, and began to lead me out to the garden. Maybe it was in English, but I hoped not.

I had not seen the garden area on first entering, and yet now it seemed to hold the entire place. I had looked only straight ahead in this place, and not to the right or to the left.

He stopped when I didn't quite follow, looking at my first table and the notebook I had left lying there.

"Oh, don't worry, I'll bring it," he said, but it wasn't enough. He could tell. "Oh, and don't worry, there are no bees right now. No bees and no wasps. It's not the season."

I started to follow him. I hadn't meant to be stubborn, and my standing motionless had been only a small moment, but it's true that I had just stood there.

"You'd know that if you were from here," he said, "no bees right now," and he walked to the garden without looking back.

I retrieved the notebook myself and followed him to the garden tables, which were quiet and cool in the netted mid-morning light. The sun was on the other side of the building's roof, and the birds were happy. He stood by a table and nodded to it.

I sat, but in pulling out my chair made the noise of a chair being pulled out. It's not much, but unmistakable as a noise. Some birds flew, and the nets moved a little. He had gotten the netting strung up high, over the tops of the umbrella trees, but with some netting under them as well to catch the yellow seed balls. One fell through, and bounced simply off the brick floor into the garden.

"It's too early for lunch," he said to me. "Maybe you want some coffee? Some *pan dulce*? It's fresh?"

Everything he said had a question mark, but nothing was a

question. He was already starting to walk back inside. I would have stopped him, but he was right.

Strangers had passed through town before, of course, he said. Most were confused or nervous, but some took control. Some strangers were stronger than others.

"They're the ones." He looked at me again, with that up-and-down glance, and again with his larger eye. But this time his look was a joke, and we laughed.

"I understand," I said, and I meant it. They're the ones to look out for, I supposed he was saying. I was a stranger here, after all, but I hadn't thought much of it, not in those terms. I was a stranger to this town, it was true, but I understood what he said. Be careful.

That connected us a little in the moment, enough so that when he came back with the coffee and sweet bread he sat down and joined me.

He didn't ask if I minded, and I didn't mind, but it surprised me, anyway.

"You can recognize a stranger in this town, and not because he is a stranger," said the man, and took a drink of his coffee even though it looked very hot, with enough steam to look like the hands of a ghost reaching up for him. "It won't be the person at all. Not at all. It will be how others in town treat him." With that he nodded his head, and it seemed to be him though it might as easily been the hands of the ghost making him nod like a puppet.

I thought about him sitting down with me so readily. It was, after all, friendly, but a little odd, too. This didn't seem to be what one would do with a stranger, here or anywhere else. He was acting like a friend, and I didn't know why.

But why should there be a why, I thought to myself. I should feel good. But I wasn't so sure. The whole thing was confusing.

"A stranger here, well, this is someone accorded the utmost in civility. Civility and suspicion, with nothing in between," he laughed. "I think we treat our strangers better than ourselves."

I supposed it was funny, too, and I smiled a little with him. But I was sitting in an awkward chair, and could not decide what to make of him, or of myself. Was I the stranger, or not? He gave me no time to think. This was perhaps a friendly act, not allowing me the moment it takes for cynicism to build a crust around a conversation, and then between two people.

Either he was indeed being friendly, or else in fact I was the stranger, and he was keeping me off-balance. I shrugged my shoulders, finally, to which he nodded his head. It was as if our bodies were themselves talking.

"Well, you know," he said to me, "a stranger in this town cannot simply order a meal, eat it, and be gone. The owner, well—you know, the other owners in the other places—they instead will offer this person, this stranger, the entire menu, no charge today, and a free tequila to boot. Just like that, no joke."

I looked at him. "A free choice? On the house?" Mine were real question marks.

"Not just a free choice, my friend. The whole meal. Anything on the menu." He nodded his head yes.

"I don't understand." Perhaps, I thought, it was the ghost talking, the ghost of the coffee, all steam. Maybe more than hands had entered and moved him.

"The whole menu. How will the owner know what the stranger wants if he doesn't offer him everything?" He looked at me for some sign of common sense, but threw up his hands. Just a little. It was not a rude gesture, but this small throwing up of his hands said what he felt.

"Listen," he continued. "I might offer the stranger simply a pork chop, and offer to cook it any way he pleased, and he would say thank you and eat it with a smile. But in his heart he would still be thinking about the tacos, and he would leave unhappy, even though he is made to smile, because what he really wanted was the tacos. But a free pork chop, how could he pass it up? And then what will he say to others?" With that he threw up his hands again, but not in frustration. It was more of a *ta-da*, there you are, it's as plain as the nose on your face.

I lifted my own eyebrows.

"No, my friend," he said, clearly understanding this conversation enough for the both of us. "No. Strangers cannot be trusted. That is why I offer them anything they want. For free. Absolutely. I don't want them to say bad things about me. Who knows what that would mean?" He nodded his head, not one way or the other, but it moved.

"I see," I said, but I was just being polite. I didn't really see at all.

"Well, it is a good thing, then. Take us, for instance. I haven't seen you around here before, but since you understand, now I know I can trust you. So then, will you want some lunch? It's not too expensive. I'll make some tacos. After the sweet breads you don't want anything too heavy. I'll go make some?"

With that he was gone, and I was left with my cooler coffee. I hadn't planned to stay for lunch, but now I was obligated. I wasn't sure how I was obligated, exactly, but I was sure that I was.

When the owner brought the tacos out I asked him how he knew I would like them.

"But who doesn't," he said, and went off to serve the others who were now gathering in the restaurant.

That seemed to be that.

I had come to town to look for family, for ancestors, really, and this man, Don Francisco, as it turns out, would have been a perfect starting point. But what I was doing here never came up. He never quite asked me, and I never quite said.

I had thought to tell him in the beginning, when he gave me a chance in the conversation, but then I thought the better of it. He was too good a starting point. I knew he would know.

That was the problem. He seemed to know everything, and I wasn't sure I liked that. He made it all easy, and it was easy, and should have been easy, but still, when something actually works that way, you get suspicious.

I don't know how to explain myself in that moment, but that other language was at work between us. It was my body talking. And it never asked Don Francisco about my family. I would ask somebody else. That's all there was to it, whether I agreed with my body or not. The words just never came out.

I should stop for a moment and say that I liked the man, a great deal, and I liked this place. It was all, in its way, perfect. And what went into my mouth in this late morning was more arresting than anything I could bring out.

The tacos were fine, crisp with good meat. The salsa, I could taste, was something made today, and fit the taste of the tacos like a meeting of primary colors, a perfect blue and a perfect yellow making a fine green. It was elemental and sure, this taste and this meal, a small alchemy with each bite.

Maybe I was just hungry, or maybe the embrace of the trees and the treble notes of the birds affected me more than I could know, but this food simply tasted sound. Complete. There was nothing else to say. This couch needed no doily. I was tired and I sat down and I felt good. That's the kind of tacos they were.

I had work to do, however, and could not stay here all day. Nothing was making me leave, and I had no real desire to leave, and I suspected I would just be coming back, but *I have work to do* is just the kind of thing one says, anyway. Who knows why. It was just time to go.

Don Francisco had by this time already brought me two Tecates with lime and another coffee. I was enjoying myself too much. That was the thing.

"How much do I owe you?" I asked him as he passed by. He stopped and added something on his fingers.

"Eleven dollars, American."

"Eleven," I repeated, and started to move my hand to my wallet. *Eleven,* said my brain, was not too cheap, but neither was it the most I had ever paid.

My body echoed, *Eleven,* but didn't understand one way or the other. It would have paid any amount of money for those two hours of life. But it was my body as well telling me to leave.

I pushed my chair out, making that sound of chairs again, but this time it felt right. It was a rhyme sound, so that if the first moment had begun my visit here, then this sound ended it. I paid Don Francisco the eleven dollars, and left another dollar and a half on the table.

He said thank you with a nod of his head and I walked out of the restaurant. I thought I was a stranger walking into the place, but it looked like I had to pay for my meal, anyway. On the one hand, that should have made me feel good. That I was a friend.

On the other hand, there was no other hand. Don Francisco

was sitting on it.

Still, the time had come for doing what I had come to do. I walked into the street to cross it, but I turned and looked back at the restaurant. It was called El Primo. I stood there looking at the sign until a car honked at me and made me jump back onto the sidewalk in front of the restaurant.

El Primo. It can mean *the first,* or *the foremost,* or anything like that. But it also means *the cousin.* And in that moment my whole lunch shouted up to me from my stomach. It was not a bad shout, but it was a noise.

It was some chemistry, some magnetism. My body knew. If opposites attract, similars repel. This is what my body felt, even if my brain thought otherwise. This is why I felt I had to leave. My body felt the greater thing. It knew pure and simple this man was my family.

Oh no, I thought, before anything else, but I didn't know why I thought that. I just knew it was the right thing to think. The two words rhymed like the pulling out and pushing in of the chair. *Oh no* and Don Francisco. They were the fitting words all right. Not reasonable, but absolute. Something indeed from magnetism.

I should have been happy, of course. Everything in the bar had been wonderful. Don Francisco was a charming host, and, perhaps, along his lines of reasoning, a friend of sorts, already. This was a good day. A good morning turning into a good day. I pulled myself up, took a breath to quiet my lunch, and walked straight back into the place.

But my body said *Oh no* louder. It said the words, and somehow they got stuck in its mouth, like a strand of food in the teeth. There was no reason for the words. But so what.

"Don Francisco," I said as I entered, just as easy and as straight as words can be. "Don Francisco."

"My friend," he said, in just the same manner. We both meant them, but our bodies were shaking their heads. It wasn't a shaking side to side in a *no,* not exactly, but neither was it precisely a *yes.* It was just a shaking. Maybe it was the ghosts. Our ghosts.

"I hope I can indeed count you as my friend, Don Francisco." I cleared my throat. "I need your help."

"Whatever I can do, of course," he said, very quickly.

It was hard for me to believe his answer. It seemed as if he had not had time to digest what he had heard. That he had given his answer just as a reflex, *a sus ordenes.* At your service. Just like that. The way he would say to anybody.

"Don Francisco, am I a stranger to you?" I asked him just in this way because I didn't know how else to begin.

"Well, no, we're old friends now, aren't we? And you did pay your bill, after all. We don't let strangers do that, do we?"

"Don Francisco, please listen. I have something serious to ask."

"Of course you might be that kind of stranger who pays his bill just to throw me off the track. That might be." He cocked his head.

"Don Francisco, I'm looking for my family."

He raised his arms as if to hug me. "Son!"

He said this, and then started laughing. It made me take a small step backward.

But he waved me back toward him. "It's just that you look so serious," he said, and stopped the joke. "All right, tell me, then, your family—when did you lose them?"

With this I let out my breath, not able to get him to understand because I wanted to say everything at once, but all the words together did not fit through the mouth. I made a small sound instead. But he understood, and he walked me to a near table, pulling out a chair. There was the sound again, but this time almost clean, almost exactly what had come out of me.

"I've come to look for family. Ancestors. Cousins. Anybody. Like that. Do you know what I mean?" The real words in order sounded anticlimactic. Why was that so difficult to say? I wondered. And to a stranger, after all. That was the truth of it.

"Oh sure, I understand perfectly," said Don Francisco. "Ancestors." He pointed to some pictures hung in a corner of the room, toward the end of the counter, along with a picture of the Virgin and John Kennedy and the old pope, John.

"Like those," he said. "I have plenty. Do you want some?"

"Don Francisco, listen. I do want some. It's not a joke. I've come all the way to find out. My Spanish is maybe not so good, I know, but I come from the Calderón family—do you know them?" I looked at him with my eyes, but I could tell that my eyes were already doing their own work. They told him I was serious. Eyes can be used, but they have a mind of their own.

"Okay. I understand. I myself am Francisco Ríos de Calderón. I know the family as well as I know my mother, God bless her."

"Stop it, Don Francisco, please." I didn't want him to tease me, not anymore.

"It's true, though. That's who I am."

"Well," I said, looking at him a little harder, "I know the family has a Francisco."

"Doesn't every family?" He laughed again in spite of everything. Don Francisco had a helper who must have come to work just in the few minutes I had gone out of the restaurant, and Don Francisco signaled him to bring us some beers.

"But I don't think it's me you're looking for. I'm Ríos de Calderón. You're talking about Francisco Calderón, just like that, on his father's side, not his mother's side like me."

"Oh," I said. It was all I could think of. When the beer came, I took a good drink. I noticed, when the helper opened them, a kind of steam came out of the beer, too, like the coffee. A spray, and then a steam, something out of the cold. What is with this place? I thought.

"I was named after him, though. Don Pancho was my uncle, I think. You know, it was so long ago, uncle or cousin, it was something like that. Do you know what I mean?" Don Francisco took a drink of his own beer.

"Would that make us cousins, then? Or something?" I had come to the right place, after all.

"Well, I count as cousins those who aren't about to ask me for something."

"I just want to know more. That's all."

"They all say that, my friend. I would have thought the less of you if you did not lie to me a little, like that. I think you have just been promoted. But all right. I'll tell you something.

"The chairs and tables outside. They're from my house when I was growing up. Your grandmother and grandfather sat in them. Your *nana* and *tata*. In fact, it was your *nana*'s hairnet, the one she always wore after your *tata* died, that gave me the idea for what to do in the garden outside."

With that he began to talk a little faster. It was the beer, the good coldness of the beer, or me, or the remembering of the detail—whatever it was, it made him talk faster. I couldn't follow everything, but when I was stuck he put his hand on my arm and got a big smile on his face. It was okay.

"And the salsa, did you like it? That was hers. I learned it from her. She used to make it many years ago when I first opened this place."

"Yes, wonderful, Don Francisco, it's wonderful. What else can you tell me?" I really was smiling. Something was letting go, something I could feel.

Don Francisco said a few more things, pointing to an old hatrack and some curtains. Then we got up to look at the pictures.

"She was beautiful," he said, and pointed at my grandmother. "I don't have any pictures of the *señor* here," he said. "But maybe tonight we'll find one."

I looked at the picture. She was beautiful, despite the wan curtain used as background. I had seen enough of these pictures by now to recognize how the photographers would use anything as backdrop, regardless of its condition. What mattered was the subject, of course. And there she was, in a jet-satin hat and some lipstick, which had been colored in.

"That's not her," I said.

Don Francisco looked at me. "What do you mean? Look again. Maybe you've seen some other pictures of her and she just looks different here. That's it. Look in this light over here," he said, and took the picture off its hanger to hold it up to the window.

"No, it's not." I looked at it for a long time. There was no question.

"But you've tricked me," said Don Francisco. He looked at me hard, with edges. He didn't want to look at me that way, I could tell, but his eyes were doing what they wanted and his bones at the joints of his elbows flexed to a point.

"No, no, Don Francisco. I didn't trick you. This just isn't her." And it wasn't. Maybe I had explained myself badly, awkwardly, with the wrong words. But it wasn't her. We both could see that now.

· · ·

"But you made me remember her. You made me tell you. What is this all about? Who are you?" He sat back in his chair and tried to fold his arms, but they fell out of their own knot, and fell a little into his lap. They, too, were doing their own work. They were telling the truth.

As was Don Francisco. But so was I. I told him everything I knew. And he told me everything he knew. But it wasn't right. It was close for a long time, but it wasn't right.

We talked a little more, and I shrugged my shoulders. I hadn't meant to upset this man who had been only kind to me. Who could have suspected he would feel this way? Don Francisco kept shaking his head a little in a *no*. He didn't say the word, but it's what he meant. He had given something away, or had let me see, something that was not mine.

He pointed me to the church. "That's where the records are," he said. "And over there is the cemetery. Good luck." He wished me good luck, and he meant the words, but it was with a tempered spirit.

I should have been the one to feel that way, and I did. But he felt it so much that it crowded into me, until I was feeling him feeling this disillusionment. Disillusionment is not the right word. It was something much bigger, and spelled much smaller. It was a real feeling more than a word.

We parted at the door to the restaurant. Afternoon had come and was honking to take me away like a taxi. The bright afternoon light is sometimes like that, especially when you want to be back inside taking a nap in the home of a friend. In the home of a cousin, just for the afternoon.

"Strangers," said Don Francisco as one of his last words, but he said the word more with his larger eye, which sometimes not only has a mind but a voice. He said it and then he gave a laugh. But it was only half a laugh. I wanted to make up the difference, but I couldn't.

"Well, you've been the best stranger, anyway," he said. "I played a joke on you, and you played a joke on me. Even?" It was not a real question, the same way he had done at the beginning of the day. With that he shook my hand.

"I'll see you," I said, but realized that these words might not be true. Maybe he was right, I thought, about believing strangers. He was right about everything else. What had I done to him?

I didn't know why he got so upset. I thought it was a small thing, the asking of a question and the giving of an answer, but I was wrong. I was wrong this time.

Maybe it was something in my Spanish, in the way I said or understood words. Some things don't travel well between languages. But perhaps it was simpler. Maybe it was just a gauge of meaning, so much about how he had loved this woman, and how he missed her, and tried to keep her in all of her ways.

Maybe it was as simple as that. The feeling belonged to him. And for a moment, maybe there was someone else. It happens with a lot of things.

I didn't know if I was a stranger or a friend, finally. Or what he was to me. Even though all the names were true for both of us, he wasn't finally my cousin, if you believed the church.

I didn't say anything else as we parted, of course. Just a small wave goodbye. I don't know if it was enough.

CONTRIBUTORS' NOTES

Ploughshares · Spring 1994

SHERMAN ALEXIE is a Spokane/Coeur d'Alene Indian and the author of five books, including *First Indian on the Moon*, a poetry collection (Hanging Loose Press), and *The Lone Ranger and Tonto Fistfight in Heaven*, a collection of short stories (Grove/Atlantic Press). His work has appeared in *Esquire, Story, The Kenyon Review, The New York Times Sunday Magazine,* and elsewhere. His first novel, *Coyote Springs,* is due out from Grove/Atlantic in the spring of 1995. **S. BEN-TOV**'s first book of poems is *During Ceasefire,* published by Harper & Row. A scholarly book, *The Artificial Paradise,* is forthcoming in Michigan University Press's series of Studies in Literature and Science. She lives in Israel part of the time and teaches creative writing at Bowling Green State University. **DANA BOUSSARD,** a nationally known artist, works and lives on a ranch near Missoula, Montana, with her husband and daughter. She has exhibited extensively, and over fifty of her works have been commissioned for state and corporate buildings. She has also illustrated several publications, including *Fools Crow* and *Killing Custer* by James Welch. (Ed. Note: *Spirit Connection,* which measures 45″ x 73″, is not represented fully on the cover.) **KEVIN BOWEN** is Director of the William Joiner Center for the Study of War and Social Consequences at the University of Massachusetts/Boston. *Playing Basketball with the Viet Cong,* his first book, will be published by Curbstone Press in the fall. **RAFAEL CAMPO,** a recipient of Boston University's Starbuck Fellowship in Poetry and *The Kenyon Review*'s Emerging Writer of the Year Award, is a resident in Internal Medicine at the University of California, San Francisco. His first manuscript, entitled *The Other Man Was Me,* won the 1993 National Poetry Series open competition and is due out this summer. **RICHARD CHESS**'s first book of poems, *Tekiah,* will be published this fall by the University of Georgia Press. He has published poems and essays in *Poetry, The American Poetry Review, The Massachusetts Review, Tikkun,* and other journals. "Tzimtzum" was composed for a "blessing way," or pre-birth ceremony, for Debi Miles and Marc Rudow, whose third son, Dovid, was born on Rosh Hashanah, 1992. **SHARON CUMBERLAND** is completing a Ph.D. in English at the City University of New York. Her poems have appeared in *The Beloit Poetry Journal, Fresh Ground, The Iowa Review, The Mickle Street Review, Poet Lore, Contact II,* and elsewhere. She once tried her vocation in an Anglican religious order. **GINA DORCELY** is a poet, translator, and essayist currently at work on a group memoir of Haitian life, *Unravelling Midnight: Truth and Experience in a Haitian Family.* She is a member of the Darkroom Collective. **JOSEPH DUEMER** is the editor of *Poets Reading Stevens* (1993), a special issue of *The Wallace Stevens Journal,* for which he serves as poetry editor. *Customs,* a collection of poems, was published in 1987 by the University of Georgia Press. Recent work appears in *The American Poetry Review, Yellow Silk, The Iowa Review,* and *The New England Review.* **DEBRA EARLING** is a member of the Confederated Salish & Kootenai Tribes of the Flathead Reservation in Northwest Montana. She holds a joint appointment in English and Native American Studies at the University of Montana in Missoula. She has just completed her novel, *Perma Red.* **ANITA ENDREZZE** is half-Yaqui and half-European (Slovenian, north Italian, and German-Romanian). Her book of poems, *at the helm of twilight* (Broken Moon Press), won the 1992 Bumbershoot-Weyerhaeuser Award and a 1993 Governor's Writer's Award. Short stories appear in two anthologies: *Talking Leaves* and *Earth Song, Sky Spirit.* "Ponies Gathering in the Dark" is from a novel-in-progress. **TED GENOWAYS**'s first chapbook, *Bullroarer,* is forthcoming from Brooding Heron Press in 1995. His poems have appeared in or are forthcoming from *Amelia, Midwest Quarterly, The Cape Rock, Poem,* and *Southern Poetry Review.* He is the editor of *Burning the Hymnal: The Uncollected Poems of William Kloefkorn* (Slow Tempo Press). **DIANE GLANCY** teaches Native American literature and creative writing at Macalester College in St. Paul. Her fourth collection of poems, *Lone Dog's Winter Count,* was published by West End Press. Her collection of essays, *Claiming Breath* (Univ. of Nebraska Press), won a 1993 American Book Award. Her fiction collections are *Firesticks* (Univ. of Oklahoma Press) and *Trigger Dance* (Univ. of Colorado and Fiction Collective II). **PATRICIA GOEDICKE**'s most recent book of poetry is *Paul Bunyan's Bearskin.* Her volume of new and selected work, *The Tongues We Speak,* was awarded *The New York Times*'s 1990 Notable Book Award. A recent recipient of a Rockefeller Foundation Residency at the Villa Serbelloni in Bellagio, Italy, she teaches poetry at the University of Montana. **JEFFREY GREENE** is the author of *To the Left of the Worshiper* (Alice James Books, 1991). He was a "Discovery"/*The Nation* Award winner and a recipient of a Connecticut Commission on the Arts grant. His poems have appeared in *Boulevard, The New Yorker, Poetry, Southwest Review,* and *Pequod.* **ANN HARLEMAN**'s collection, *Happiness,* just out from the University of Iowa Press, won the 1993 John Simmons Short Fiction Award. She is working on a novel about her great-grandfather, who murdered for love. **MARGARET KAUFMAN** received an M.F.A. from Warren Wilson in 1993. Awarded a 1993 Marin Arts Council poetry grant, she lives in Kentfield, California. *Aunt Sallie's Lament* (The Janus Press, 1988) has been recently issued in a trade edition by Chronicle Books. "Lot's Wife" is part of her new manuscript, *"No" in Every Step.* **MARSHALL N. KLIMASEWISKI**'s short stories have been published in *The New Yorker, The Antioch Review, Quarterly West,* and a 1988 issue of *Ploughshares* dedicated to "Fiction Discoveries." A story entitled "JunHee" was anthologized in *Best American Short Stories, 1992.* He is at work on a novel and a collection of stories. **MARK LEVINE**'s book, *Debt,* is available from William Morrow. He received a Whiting Writer's Award in 1993 and will be the Hodder Fellow at Princeton University in 1994-95. **PETER MARCUS** has poems in *Agni, The Iowa Review, The North American Review, Poetry, Poetry East, Willow Springs,* and elsewhere. He lives in Flagstaff, Arizona, working as a therapist at

Northern Arizona University, where his main interests are counseling Native American students and students with eating disorders. TED MCNULTY, an Irish-American poet living in Dublin, won the Hennessy Literary Prize as "New Irish Writer of the Year." His work has appeared in *The Observer, The Spectator, Oxford Poetry,* and *The Irish Times. Rough Landings,* his current collection, was published by Salmon Poetry/Poolbeg Press. SCOTT MOMADAY is the author of *The Ancient Child, The Names, The Way to Rainy Mountain,* and *House Made of Dawn,* which won the Pulitzer Prize in 1969. LEE ANN MORTENSEN recently won a fiction fellowship from the *Poets & Writers* exchange program. She teaches writing and literature at Utah Valley State College. Her writing has appeared in *Mississippi Review, Quarterly West, Inscape,* and *The Student Review.* "Not Quite Peru" is the first chapter to be published from her nearly completed novel, *Strip.* THYLIAS MOSS's most recent books were both published in 1993: *Small Congregations,* a volume of new and selected poems, and *I Want to Be,* a book for children. Currently she teaches at the University of Michigan and lives in Ann Arbor with her husband and their two young sons. Coming soon is a second children's book, *Somewhere Else Right Now.* OPHELIA NAVARRO, a native of Tucson, Arizona, is an undergraduate student at Wellesley College. She is working on a collection of short stories and a play. This is the first time her work has appeared in print. SIMON ORTIZ's new collection of poetry, *After and Before the Lightning,* will be published by the University of Arizona Press in the fall. Previous poetry works include *From Sand Creek* and *Woven Stone.* He has also published short fiction, *Fightin': New & Collected Stories,* and children's literature, *The People Shall Continue.* Currently living in Tucson, Arizona, he served in the 1980s as Interpreter and First Lt. Governor of Acoma Pueblo, his Native American community. EILEEN POLLACK is the author of *The Rabbi in the Attic,* a collection of short fiction published in 1991 by Delphinium/Simon & Schuster. Two previous stories have appeared in *Ploughshares,* and one subsequently was awarded a Pushcart Prize; the other received the Cohen Award. She teaches at Emerson College and at Tufts University in Boston. ALBERTO ALVARO RÍOS's most recent book is *Teodoro Luna's Two Kisses,* published by W.W. Norton. Other books include *The Lime Orchard Woman, The Iguana Killer,* and *Whispering to Fool the Wind.* The recent recipient of the Arizona Governor's Arts Award, he edited the Spring 1992 issue of *Ploughshares* and is currently Professor of English at Arizona State University. A new book of short stories, *Pig Cookies,* is forthcoming from San Francisco: Chronicle in 1995. NATASHA SAJE's collection of poems, *Red Under the Skin,* winner of the 1993 Agnes Lynch Starrett Prize, will be published by the University of Pittsburgh Press in the fall of 1994. With Barbara Bryan, she is editing an anthology of South Slav–American writing that explores ethnicity and nationalism. RIPLEY SCHEMM lives in Missoula, Montana, and teaches throughout the state for the Montana Arts Council. She has poems forthcoming in *Circle of Women: An Anthology of Western Women Writers,* due from Viking Press this year. DIANN BLAKELY SHOAF's first volume of poems, *Hurricane Walk,* was published in 1992 by BOA Editions. Work from a new manuscript, *Not a Stranger,* has appeared or is forthcoming in *Denver Quarterly, Harvard Magazine, The Nation, Ploughshares,* and *The Southern Review.* **BRUCE SMITH** is the author of three books of poetry, *The Common Wages* (Sheep Meadow, 1983), *Silver and Information* (Univ. of Georgia Press, 1985), and, most recently, *Mercy Seat* (Univ. of Chicago Press, 1994). **CHARLES H. WEBB**'s collection of poetry, *Everyday Outrages,* was published by Red Wind Books. He edited *Stand Up Poetry: The Anthology,* which has just been published by the University Press, CSU Long Beach. **ELIZABETH WOODY**'s poetry collection *Hand Into Stone* received an American Book Award from the Before Columbus Foundation in 1990, and an expanded edition is forthcoming from Eighth Mountain Press in late 1994. A new collection, *Luminaries of the Humble,* will be available from the University of Arizona Press in the fall. A Yakima, Warm Springs, Wasco, and Navajo Indian, Woody is an enrolled member of the Confederated Tribes of the Indian Reservation at Warm Springs, Oregon. **JUDITH YAMAMOTO**'s poetry has appeared or is forthcoming in *Magic Realism, Quanta, Artmeis, Southern Poetry Review, Partisan Review,* and other literary magazines. *Redbook* published a short story of hers, "A Long Time to Be Gone," which was included in Martha Foley's 1974 Distinctive Short Stories List. **SUSAN YUZNA** grew up in Minnesota, received her B.A. from the University of Iowa, and is now in the M.F.A. program at the University of Montana. Her poems are forthcoming in *The North Stone Review, The Antioch Review,* and *The Laurel Review.* She lives in Missoula with her son and her dog.

ABOUT JAMES WELCH

Ploughshares · Spring 1994

James Welch refers to himself as an Indian—not a Native American, not an American Indian—and he is often amused that, while the simple ethnic designation is used as a matter of course on reservations, it causes a furor on university campuses. Part Blackfeet, part Gros Ventre, with some Irish mixed in, Welch has always been concerned with the place given to Indians in American society, and he has made it his lifework as a writer to illuminate the richness of his culture and the heartache of its dislocation.

Yet being a writer—much less being credited, alongside Scott Momaday, as a forerunner of the Native American literary renaissance—was the last thing Welch could have imagined for himself as he grew up in Montana, where he has lived nearly all of his life. He was born in 1940 in the town of Browning, and raised on the Blackfeet and Fort Belknap Indian reservations, only leaving the state to attend high school in Minneapolis, where his father worked briefly as a welder. Despite the extreme poverty around him, Welch remembers his childhood with fondness—particularly the beauty of the Montana landscape and the physical labors of feeding and putting up hay on the cattle ranch and farm that his father ran for a time. Admittedly, he was not a very ambitious kid, and he thought he would eventually get some sort of government job, similar to his mother's stints as a stenographer for the Bureau of Indian Affairs, or his father's work as a hospital administrator for the Indian Health Service, or his brother's job as a forester—something, Welch says, "where you didn't have to display a lot of originality." He was a mediocre student, preferring sports to studying, and he didn't read much, other than comic books and the occasional Western (Welch, like other Indians on his reservation, always cheered on the white heroes in cowboy and Indian movies, never seeing any irony in it). But in high school, Welch found a hobby, an avocation, as a closet poet. A teacher required her class to memorize a poem every week, and

Welch began writing his own—imitations of "Gungha Din" and "a lot of mushy love poetry and nature poetry about the stately pines." He kept the poems in a notebook, never showing them to anyone, afraid of being teased. "I wrote a lot of them in study hall to while away the hours," he says, "and I would always have one hand over what I'd written."

After two years at Northern Montana College, he transferred to the University of Montana. There, he took a short story course on a whim, and he found he wanted to take more. The university had just started offering an M.F.A. degree in creative writing, and Welch decided to apply, not knowing what else to do. His grades were terrible, but he was admitted because there were so few applicants. He enrolled in a poetry workshop conducted by Richard Hugo, whom Welch extols as a master teacher, a sensation: "I was so inspired by him that I just kept writing."

Welch and Hugo became fast friends, and one afternoon, they went on an ice fishing trip together with J. D. Reed. They stopped by a bar in the town of Dixon afterwards, and under the influence of a few drinks, they exuberantly challenged one another to write a poem about the bar. They set a deadline of two weeks, and pledged that the three poems had to be published simultaneously in one magazine. "The title of the poems was 'The Only Bar in Dixon,'" Welch recalls. "Somehow we sent it out to *The New Yorker* on a fluke, and they took them and printed all three in the same issue." Thus began Welch's somewhat improbable career as a poet.

He was lucky enough to have a wife, Lois, who agreed to support his endeavors, and while she taught in the English department at the University of Montana (she now directs the creative writing program), he worked on his poems. In 1971, he published his first collection, *Riding the Earthboy 40*, a title which referred to the forty acres of land adjacent to his parents' ranch, leased from a family named the Earthboys. The volume, especially when it was revised and reissued by Harper & Row in 1976, was very well-received, drawing admiration for the melding of Blackfeet visions and dreams with surrealistic techniques, as well as for his descriptions of contemporary life for Indians in Montana, their detachment from their tribal past and their concomitant clashes with

PHOTO: MARC A. HEFTY

the surrounding white world, which would become a consistent theme for Welch. "The townspeople outside the reservations had a very superior attitude toward Indians," he says, "which was kind of funny, because they weren't very wealthy; they were on the fringes of society themselves. But nobody would take checks from Indians, nobody would give them any credit, and nobody would let them drink in the bars. There was a rudeness, a brusqueness, with which the Indians were treated constantly. At a very young age, that had entered my consciousness."

As much as Welch appreciated the reception of his book, one thing irked him: nearly all of the critics emphasized the "bleakness" of Montana when addressing his poems, a common perception of the land he loves. Perhaps the vast distances between towns and people create a feeling of isolation, Welch admits, but the scenery itself is majestic. "So many people who come to northern Montana tell me," Welch says, "without realizing that it's insulting, that they drove like hell to get to the mountains, because the plains are so boring. It's amazing to me that people don't take the time to get off the highway and really notice what's there. I guess their idea of beauty is too inflexible." He began writing a long poem, a travelogue of sorts, listing Montana's virtues, but as he went along, he became interested in delving into a narrative about the state's inhabitants, and he turned the poem into a novel, *Winter in the Blood.* He showed it to his friend, the writer William Kittredge, who found something wrong on every page. "We stayed up one whole night, and he pointed out all these things to me, and of course I was discouraged and put it away."

Shortly thereafter, Welch's wife took a leave of absence, and they spent a year in Greece, where Welch doggedly revised the book. In the meantime, Ted Solotaroff, the prominent Harper & Row editor, called Dick Hugo, scouting around for novels. "I think Jim Welch is working on one," Hugo told him. "He took one with him."

Solotaroff published *Winter in the Blood* in 1974. In it, a nameless Indian narrator flounders on a reservation, and is only able to attain a sense of identity when learning the names and history of his grandparents. A second novel, *The Death of Jim Loney,* followed in 1979, and portrays a "half-breed" with a similar existential crisis, haunted by a biblical passage and an image of a black bird, which in Indian tradition presages a benevolent, guiding spirit or, alternately, a warning. But Loney cannot interpret either symbol, alienated as he is from both white and Indian cultures. The two novels are written with a spare, episodic style, laden with absurdism and black humor, and share a narrative arc that requires the characters' return to the reservation, and hence to their ancestral pasts, for them to find any meaning in their lives.

Welch himself does not discount the possibility of assimilation, but he acknowledges the difficulty of it, and he encourages the neo-tribalism that has developed in recent years. "Before, Indian people had been so defeated, they were always looking for outsiders, for the government, to somehow come in and fix things," he says. "But now, they seem to realize that they're the only ones who can save themselves. The economic piece is still missing, since it's so hard to attract industry to reservations, but spiritually and educationally, they're doing just fine. Each tribe has a community college now, and they teach the language, they teach the traditions."

Welch returned to his own traditions in the novel *Fools Crow,* which was released in 1986 and chosen as the year's best work of fiction by *The Los Angeles Times*. The book is a historical record of a Pikuni Blackfeet tribe that was massacred at the Marias River by white settlers in 1870. One hundred seventy-three Indians, mostly women and children, were killed, but among those who escaped was Welch's great-grandmother, of whom Welch heard stories from his father. Virtually nothing tangible about the incident had survived. Even the site of the massacre was unknown until Welch, his wife, and several friends located it, with a photograph as their single clue. *Fools Crow* focuses on the coming of age of White Man's Dog, who grows into a hunter, warrior, and healer. He is renamed Fools Crow and is on the verge of becoming a great leader of the Pikuni. But with the advent of the repeating rifle, the buffalo herds are disappearing, and the Indians are being eliminated just as quickly by smallpox and the U.S. Army. Fools Crow is given the responsibility of foreseeing and witnessing the cultural genocide of his tribe.

Evoking the tribe's way of life proved to be a challenge for Welch. Not only did he have to research small, everyday details, like how the Blackfeet tanned hides and performed ceremonies of worship, he also had to make their belief system plausible—the visions, superstitions, prayers, and ghosts—a considerable task, since Welch was raised as a Catholic and now calls himself an agnostic. "I do believe in the viability of Indian spiritualism, however," Welch says. "Even though in a lot of Indian societies, it's in danger of being lost, or has been lost, I think it's still the best way of looking at the world for Indians—better than any organized religion in this country" (there are quite a few *fundamentalist* Native Americans, Welch reports, who believe that tribal religions are pagan).

Welch's fourth novel, *The Indian Lawyer* (1990), forced him to confront his political beliefs. If he had received any criticism from Native Americans during his career, it was that he had not presented any contemporary role models in his books, as he never shied away from the alcoholism and violence on reservations. So he created Sylvester Yellow Calf—college basketball star, Stanford Law School graduate, partner in a Helena law firm, and candidate for Congress. Yellow Calf also serves on a parole board, and is seduced by an inmate's wife and then blackmailed. Welch himself served on a parole board for ten years. A friend, the dean of the University of Montana law school, called him one day and asked if he wanted to be appointed to the board. Welch first told her no, but she convinced him. "If you don't do it," she said, "some redneck rancher from eastern Montana will." The experience was rewarding for Welch in many ways: "In the general population of Montana, it's about seven to eight percent Indian. But the population in prison is always between twenty and twenty-five percent Indian. I think I helped some of the other board members understand Indians better. One of their attitudes had been not to return Indians to the reservation, because that might encourage them to get into trouble again. But sending them to Billings or Great Falls or wherever, without a tribal support system, would only guarantee trouble." Yet the years of service took a toll on Welch. He was frequently depressed after hearings and had nightmares. "When I first got on the board, I was kind of a flaming liberal, and I didn't think anyone was inherently bad. But after you meet some of these inmates who'd committed violent or deviant acts and you read their psychological evaluations, you conclude that there are some people who are just plain evil."

As a change of pace, Welch switched to historical nonfiction for his next book, *Killing Custer*, which will be published by W.W. Norton in October. Leading up to the Massacre at Wounded Knee in 1890, it explores the post–Civil War period of western expansion, told mostly from the Sioux and Cheyenne points of view. In addition, a quarter of the book is from Welch's perspective, plumbing his personal ruminations as he watched the filming of the PBS documentary *Last Stand at Little Big Horn*, which he had co-written.

Welch has some ambivalence about the continual pressure on him to be a Native American spokesman. "I used to object to being called an Indian writer, and would always say I was a writer who happened to be an Indian, and who happened to write about Indians. I think ethnic and regional labels are insulting to writers and really put restrictions on them. People don't think your work is quite as universal." Sometimes, he wishes he could write as he does now in his house in Missoula, working in afternoon and late-night shifts, but feel free to do any story he wanted, one set in

Seattle, say, which touches on Indians only peripherally. On the other hand, he accepts the necessity of clarifying and debunking stereotypes. "Most people in America have a clichéd idea of Indians, that they're all alcoholics and lazy and on welfare. Maybe through literature, people can gain an understanding of how Indians got the way they are today, and how they differ from one another, as tribes and as individuals." Besides, the history and culture of Indians are endlessly fascinating to Welch. "I'd like to explore as much of it as I can, each piece of it," he says, "and of course that will take me the rest of my life to do."

—*Don Lee*

1-800-HOT-RIBS *Poems by Catherine Bowman. Gibbs Smith, $9.95 paper. Reviewed by Diann Blakely Shoaf.*

"I want words meat-hooked from the living steer," Lowell wrote, as if foreseeing *1-800-HOT-RIBS*, the debut collection by Catherine Bowman, a skilled young poet who seems to manipulate the language with a branding iron in one hand and a bullwhip in the other. Bowman's native soil is Texas, and though she casts a cold eye on its codes of Bubba Machismo and Cheerleader Femininity, she knows that denying one's roots is equivalent to using a butcher's cleaver to perform an act of self-amputation. She also knows how thin the line between Bubba and the Cheerleader really is.

In "Dove at Sundown," for example, she writes of herself and another female hunter: "We clean our kill by headlight. First you twist / the head off like a bottle cap. The thumb / and pointer finger are used as hooks / to disengage guts and any shot." Once the birds are eaten, the women "strip down and soak / in a cleaned-out cow tank swimming pool," watching bombers from a nearby Air Force base "out for test flights: slow and prehistoric, / petroglyphs of winged jaguars come to life."

"Dove at Sundown" is written in rough blank verse, and Bowman is particularly adept in the use of traditional forms. Her kinetic vernacular and jazzy rhythms, which can seem fey and unshaped in the few poems where they lack a counterbalancing tension, are perhaps most successful in sonnets like "Jackie in California" and "LBJ Ranch Barbeque" or in the several sestinas here, "Spice Night" being another of the delights Bowman's book offers.

This last poem is set in San Antonio, home of the Alamo, whose suicidal defense is accorded a special place in Texas lore. Bowman has cheerfully pillaged that lore, and our national stock of myths and archetypes as well, for *1-800-HOT-RIBS*, a book whose tongue-in-cheek bravado and linguistic swagger will conquer, I predict, the hearts of many readers.

Diann Blakely Shoaf is a regular reviewer for the "Bookshelf." Her collection of poems, Hurricane Walk, *was published by BOA Editions in 1992.*

RISE THE EUPHRATES *A novel by Carol Edgarian. Random House, $22.00 cloth. Reviewed by Don Lee.*

It is an Armenian tradition to begin the telling of a story with the words *Gar oo chugar:* There was and there was not. The phrase is repeated throughout Carol Edgarian's exquisitely written first novel, *Rise the Euphrates,* and it is a fitting refrain for this story of three Armenian-American women and the shame that both binds and divides them.

The majority of the novel portrays the coming of age of Seta Loon, but she serves as a wonderfully lyrical narrator for her family's history as well, starting with her grandmother's experiences in 1915, when the massacres that would kill over a million Armenians began. Nine-year-old Casard witnesses the brutal execution of her townspeople, and then she and her mother, with several hundred children and women, are forced on a march through the desert to the Euphrates River. There, they are told to jump to their deaths into the swirling water, but Casard, in a moment of innocent hesitation, abandons her mother and survives, albeit just barely—left so shocked and ashamed, she forgets her own name.

She escapes to the U.S., where she is indiscriminately renamed, and settles in Memorial, Connecticut, marries, and has a daughter. Yet hanging on to "Old Country customs" and superstitions, Casard never speaks of the massacres, which she refers to as "the Indignities," and she instructs her progeny to follow suit: "And if asked, Where is this Armenia? Casard taught me to spit in my hand and answer, *Gunantz.* Gone." Only peripherally do her daughter, Araxie, and granddaughter, Seta, learn the secret of what Casard regards as an unpardonable betrayal—leaving her mother at the river—and her guilt casts an *anetzk,* or curse, over the family. Araxie forever possesses a melancholy that makes her defy Casard and marry George Loon, a non-Armenian, an outsider, an *odar.* And Seta—mystically beset with dreams and images of what happened at the Euphrates—must watch Casard and Araxie continue to provoke each other's wrath, never able to make peace or console their grief. Ironically, it is Seta's father, the *odar*, who best understands the family's affliction—the unimaginable choice made by the women that day in 1915 to drown their children and themselves, rather than becoming victims to the Turks, their fundamental dignity taken away, a violation that manifested itself in sadness and remained in the blood. The Armenians, in a sense, are the true *odars*, for what does it mean to be an outsider but "to lose one's country, one's family, one's hope."

It becomes Seta Loon's responsibility to end the legacy of her family's tragedies. Thirty-three now, pregnant, unmarried, she returns to Connecticut in the novel's epilogue to see her mother, knowing that "in families the worst betrayal is the withholding of forgiveness."

Rise the Euphrates is an important, powerful, poignant novel. Its minor flaws in plotting—the threads of betrayal could be more cohesive; the suspense created over the recovery of Casard's real name is misleading—are far outweighed by the book's richness and luminous prose. Carol Edgarian's prodigious talents as a storyteller, her ability to account what there was and was not for these Armenian Americans, should not be missed. "Our tales are what bind," Edgarian writes in the voice of Seta Loon, "they are the spiraling—the vicious, wondrous spiraling—which, if never questioned, lock the generations in a web of infinite expectation, lies, shame, hope. For my unborn child, I am after hope. Hope, and the chance for a new story that will put to rest the lies and shame."

THE OPEN BOAT: POEMS FROM ASIAN AMERICA *An anthology edited by Garrett Hongo. Anchor Books, $12.00 paper. Reviewed by Stewart David Ikeda.*

In this time of multicultural vogue, Garrett Hongo's extraordinary poetry anthology, *The Open Boat: Poems from Asian America*, makes an intelligent statement about the limitations of limits, the perils of essentialism, and the urgent necessity for protest art to remain dynamic. Even the shaky construct of "Asian America" itself is challenged in the anthology, for the works of these thirty-one poets defy reduction to any single, "representative" cultural beat. Readers won't find "the Asian American Experience" rendered here, but thirty-one such experiences crafted to near perfection.

And it is a distinctly American book. "We are already upon the shore," writes Hongo. More of the baby bust than boom, his generation's rootedness affords it the luxury of imaginative travel unavailable to ancestors. The poems hydroplane beyond the California-centric, immigration-era settings that have obsessed earlier writers, with younger poets such as Chicagoan Li-Young Lee maintaining only imaginative ties to Asia: "I've never been in Peking, or the Summer Palace / nor stood on the great Stone Boat to watch / the rain begin on Kuen Ming Lake." David Mura takes a haunting empathetic journey to post-Bomb Hiroshima as a radiation victim in "Hibakusha's Letter," and Jessica Hagedorn—in the voice of Yolanda, a dominatrix-missionary—airbuses to Europe ("what / a creature / all dis history / and no future") to enlighten Amsterdam with the gospel of American soul, "SOME REAL ROCK 'N' ROLL . . . SOME REAL BLACK." Like their poems, the poets themselves span and expand geographical frontiers. Whereas "Asian American" in earlier anthologies meant "West Coast Japanese, Chinese, and Filipino American," Hongo has enlisted a pleasingly motley, often multiracial crew, extending the literature's origins to uncharted lands: Kashmiri, Indian, Sri Lankan, and Indonesian America; and to even more exotic locales like Minneapolis, Chicago, and Philadelphia.

With the mixed races, geographies, and concerns of these poets, the anthology might first appear random and messy, particularly to essentialists. In addition, Hongo has "No Name Writers" rubbing elbows with Critics' Circle winners, culling their poems from literary journals, and although he yokes together old antagonists like Maxine Hong Kingston and Lawson Inada, he lifts them out of traditional contexts, rather than attempting to reignite their feud. Hongo is obviously trying to embrace younger readers as well, making the anthology intellectually and financially accessible, and contemporary without being trendy (no bug-eyed dragons smolder on its cover; it exoticizes nothing). But Hongo's organizing principles in compiling this anthology are far from whimsical, nor are they designed merely to attract a mainstream audience. While sharing a certain consciousness of history and race in America, what ultimately binds these poets together are passionate pens, a fresh perspective, and forward motion.

Asian America has long been imprisoned within a skewed history of (self-) oppression, confusion, misinterpretation; if not externally defined as peopled with yellow demons or ultra-white nerds, its obsessions often locked its imagination in internment camps and Chinatowns. Either way, "the Experience" has been read as what was *done* to Asian Americans, not what they *did*. "We write," Hongo argues, "about violence to women, about the paintings of Utamaro and Willem de Kooning, about plantation workers and picture brides, about factory work and the pleasures/dangers of sex. We write about our Eurasian children...we write about food and family, about what we hold sacred and what we deem profane."

As such, this important book contains a dazzling display of little-known personal, not collective, cultures. The diversity of these songs—sociological, cultural, political, religious, artistic—creates a fascinating American symphony in the only language equipped to convey what we direly need to know here, in America, today. In its ambitious scope and inclusiveness—its openness—*The Open Boat* sails past horizons of what American literature has been to explore what it will be.

Stewart David Ikeda had a short story included in the Spring 1993 issue of Ploughshares. *He currently lives in Madison, where he teaches creative writing and Asian American literature at the University of Wisconsin.*

A BRIEF HISTORY OF MALE NUDES IN AMERICA *Stories by Dianne Nelson. Univ. of Georgia Press, $19.95 cloth. Reviewed by Jessica Dineen.*

In *A Brief History of Male Nudes in America,* Dianne Nelson's first story collection, the element of place—a ranch in Nevada, a tent in Kansas, or a hotel in Santa Fe—is more than a backdrop for action; it is an integral part of each character's life. "A Map of Kansas," for instance, is a chilling story about a large family reunion at which the narrator's anorexic sister, Katie, has become silent and aloof; as her body grows thinner, she seems to be disappearing into the landscape: "In Kansas in the dark, my sister is all softness and memory as she sits there rehearsing the silence that will steadily grow around her. Katie—the riddleless woods, the renderless garden. Not far away, I am looking at her, thinking of her. I am listening to the crickets shape and reshape this fierce world."

Several of Nelson's characters, bogged down by familial problems, search for momentum. In the title story, a teenage girl is tired of the seemingly endless parade of men who have visited her mother. One night, after she hears her mother in bed with yet another man, she decides to run away, but then turns back: "At last I'm calm on those sidewalks, I'm limp and light. I watch my feet all the way home, step after step—no melody, no rhythm—until all I know is the beauty of my own shoes."

In one of the best stories in the collection, "Ground Rules," Lewis and his thirteen-year-old son go to the home of the woman who abandoned them three years earlier "in the unlucky state of Missouri." They believe they will get their lives back on track by stealing Lewis's toddler son. After the abduction, with both boys asleep in the car, Lewis imagines "everything they would do: ski and rebuild engines, hang a Christmas Piñata from the back tree, they would swim and cook eggs with Tabasco, grow some Indian corn. On and on it went in Lewis's mind until he grew tender with the largeness of their lives, until sometime after midnight—the boys still sleeping, the chain-link of stars glimmering above—they crossed the line into the sweet, big grainbelt of Kansas."

Nelson uses an extraordinary range of language—provincial, heightened, commonplace, metaphoric, crass—and while some passages are slightly excessive, the overall style is very effective. A down-to-earth tone prevails, aided by the fact that even Nelson's most exotic characters can speak unself-consciously about anything: sex; nudity; loving, strange, violent thoughts. These nebulous, difficult topics come to rest on the same plane with the everyday realities of living.

The narrator of "Paperweight" laments, "If it weren't for my body, I could fly." The issue for her, as for other characters, is whether she can wade through the overwhelming nuances of surface and place and ultimately ground herself. She falls in love with a man because he is increasingly *present*—"he stood complicating the darkness"—and, later, when she thinks of her body next to his, she sees "how time is a ritual, a complicated working out of who will reach over and turn the lamp off at night, of how things will finally be said and done."

CONTRIBUTOR SPOTLIGHT With the poem "The Battle Hymn of the Republic" (p. 144), Rafael Campo makes his second appearance in *Ploughshares,* but he has been a friend to the journal for many years, volunteering as a staff poetry reader from 1988-92.

JORGE ARROYO

During and since that period, Campo has established a reputation as a poet in his own right, publishing his work in magazines such as *The Paris Review, The Kenyon Review, Agni,* and *The Nation.* Last spring, his first book, *The Other Man Was Me,* was selected as a National Poetry Series winner and will be released by Arte Público Press this July. In the meantime, he graduated from Harvard Medical School and is currently a second-year resident at the University of California, San Francisco. All this, and Campo is not quite thirty years old.

Except for four years in Venezuela, Campo spent his childhood in northern New Jersey, the eldest son of a Cuban immigrant father and an Italian mother. Theirs was a close-knit, loving family, but, quite predictably, there were extraordinary pressures put on Campo to succeed. His grandfather, after escaping Franco in Spain, had been a rancher and a community leader in Cuba, supporting the revolution against Batista's corrupt regime. But once Castro took over, Campo's grandfather was thrown into jail and then had no choice but to flee the country upon his release. He worked in a New Jersey furniture factory for the rest of his life, and he saw his son, Campo's father, who had been trained as an engineer, relegated to the factory line at American Can (he rose through the ranks, and, after thirty years, is now an executive vice president). Their struggles led Campo's grandfather and father to instill a bitter pride in him; they urged him to retain the Latino culture and language they had been forced to forsake, and at the same time they insisted that he become an exemplary American, a man of respect, a doctor.

But Campo would meet resistance in pursuit of this immigrants' dream, both externally and internally. As the only minority in school, he was routinely harassed. Consequently, Campo began trying to distance himself from his heritage, assimilating as much as he could, for instance calling himself Ralph instead of Rafael. Yet it didn't work. His classmates continued to revile not only his racial and socioeconomic otherness, but also something more amorphous, something that Campo fervently wanted to deny. "My earliest attractions were to men," he says, "and I tried desperately to exorcise it from myself. I dated girls in high school and, in many ways, was sexually aggressive with them. It had a lot to do with the machismo I was brought up with, the male/female dynamics on my father's side of the family, which was very traditionally Latino."

Not surprisingly, then, Campo's interest in writing poems as an adolescent was discouraged. Although his mother was an art teacher and Latinos in general have a strong appreciation for the arts, his family viewed Campo's poetry with alarm. They felt he couldn't afford any distractions from his studies toward being a doctor, and they thought poetry might reinforce the gay impulses he seemed to possess—a subject they never discussed openly, because it was unthinkable. He wrote in secret. At Amherst College, as an undergraduate elective, he took a poetry workshop with Eve Sedgwick, and for the first time he found expression for his sexuality and his identity as a Latino American, and he ended up double-majoring in Neuroscience and English, but he still remained quiet about his writing. Even as he began publishing his work when he was in medical school, he kept his poetry concealed as a private avocation, for to do otherwise would have meant revealing to his family that he was gay.

Halfway through his M.D., however, Campo no longer could avoid the numerous issues he had, for so long, left unaddressed. First, he admitted to his parents his sexual preference, which they of course had difficulty accepting. The news was mitigated to some degree by the confession that Jorge Arroyo, whom they had come to know and love as Campo's friend of six years, was in fact his partner. Eventually, his parents were able to abide with Campo's homosexuality, but his next disclosure shocked them further: he was thinking of abandoning medicine and becoming a poet.

"My first year of taking care of patients in the wards was entirely disastrous," Campo explains. There was a paternalistic attitude at Harvard Medical School, which tried its best to shield third-year students from patients with serious diseases, particularly AIDS. Nonetheless, Campo saw that the HIV patients were disproportionately Latino and African American, and that most of them were gay. "I was suddenly being confronted with these issues of oppression, only now they were manifested in illness," he says. "It goes back to my efforts as an adolescent to be really American. Up to that point, wearing that white doctor's coat symbolized *whiteness* to me. I didn't want to be aligned with these drug addicts, these gay men, and all the stereotypes that the medical community, which is incredibly homophobic, assigns to these people. I felt alienated from both my work and my patients. I thought I had made the biggest mistake of my life. I was in a profession that not only despised who I was, it was also beating the humanity out of me."

Miserable and demoralized, Campo decided to take a year off. He was offered the prestigious George Starbuck Poetry Fellowship at Boston University, and, more to escape medicine than to pursue poetry, he went to B.U. But studying with Derek Walcott and Robert Pinsky, he discovered his way back to medicine. "In my poems, I was finding the voices of my patients telling the story of my own life, my conflicts with my sexuality and my identity as an American. It taught me more than Harvard Medical School ever did about how to take care of people." Walcott and Pinsky—along with Marilyn Hacker and the works of Thom Gunn—also reinforced Campo's penchant for formal poetry, particularly the sonnet and *terza rima*. "Rhyming recreated the musicality of Spanish for me, and I could really see the rhythms of the body's internal processes in those forms," Campo says. "After all, I was spending my whole day listening to people's hearts and lungs and their narratives as they told me the stories of their illnesses."

Campo was finally able to find a balance, a relationship, in his dual roles as physician and poet, and he finished his manuscript for *The Other Man Was Me* before returning for his fourth year of medical school. The book is divided into three sections, exploring the immigrant experience; bilingualism; the delicacy of doctor-patient relationships, especially in the time of AIDS; and Campo's patriarchal lineage, which is covered in four sonnet sequences and extends from his grandfather to his imagined son.

These days, Campo works about eighty hours a week at the University of California, San Francisco, hospital, where his partner, Jorge Arroyo, is an ophthalmologist and where another writer, Ethan Canin, is also a resident. Campo steals time between admissions to write poems and is nearly finished with his second book. In addition, he has begun writing nonfiction, and he has published two powerful essays about the human body and healing in *The Kenyon Review*. He plans to be a general internist and treat people with HIV or AIDS who don't have access to care. Ironically, being a poet, publishing a book in English, has contributed more to identifying himself as an American than being a doctor, although he has issues yet to resolve. "I'm still trying to find a way to stand alongside people and be considered an equal, somebody with a voice," he says, "and that's where I hope my book will take me."

The Other Man Was Me will be published in trade paperback on July 1 ($16.95 cloth, $8.00 paper). If you're interested in making an advance order, call Arte Público Press at 1-800-633-ARTE.

EDITORS' CORNER Some noteworthy new books by former *Ploughshares* editors: *The City Below,* James Carroll's ninth novel, which chronicles two brothers in Boston during the Kennedy years. *The Angel of History,* Carolyn Forché's full-length poem—a meditation on how memory survives the unimaginable horrors of history. *Running to Paradise: Yeats's Poetic Art,* M. L. Rosenthal's provocative readings of Yeats's lyric poetry and poetic drama.

HONORARIA Thanks to the Lannan Foundation, we have increased our honoraria to writers: $10/page for prose, $20/page for poetry, $40 minimum per title, and $200 maximum per author.

PUBLIC SERVICE ANNOUNCEMENT Poets House and Asphodel Press have published the first edition of *Directory of American Poetry Books,* an invaluable buyer's guide to books of poems released during the previous year.

—*Don Lee*

MFA

Writing Program
at Vermont College

Intensive 11-Day Residencies

July and January on the beautiful Vermont campus.
Workshops, classes, readings, conferences, followed
by **Non-Resident 6-Month Writing Projects** in
poetry and fiction individually designed during residency.
In-depth criticism of manuscripts. Sustained dialogue with faculty.

Post-Graduate Writing Semester

for those who have already finished a graduate degree
with a concentration in creative writing.

Vermont College admits students
regardless of race, creed, sex or ethnic origin.

Scholarships and financial aid available.

Faculty

Tony Ardizzone	Phyllis Barber
Robin Behn	Francois Camoin
Mark Cox	Mark Doty
Jonathan Holden	Lynda Hull
Richard Jackson	Sydney Lea
Diane Lefer	Ellen Lesser
Jack Myers	Sena Jeter Naslund
Christopher Noel	Pamela Painter
David Rivard	Mary Ruefle
Betsy Sholl	Sharon Sheehe Stark
Gladys Swan	Leslie Ullman
Roger Weingarten	W.D. Wetherell
David Wojahn	

Visiting Writers include:

Julia Alvarez	Richard Howard
Brett Lott	Naomi Shihab Nye

For more information:

Roger Weingarten, MFA Writing Program, Box 889,
Vermont College of Norwich University, Montpelier, VT 05602
802–828–8840
Low-residency B.A. and M.A. programs also available.

POETS IN PERSON

An Audio Series on American Poets and Their Art

Introduction • A. R. Ammons • John Ashbery
Gwendolyn Brooks • Rita Dove • Allen Ginsberg
Maxine Kumin • James Merrill • W. S. Merwin
Sharon Olds • Adrienne Rich • Karl Shapiro
Gary Soto • Charles Wright

Produced, written, and hosted by Joseph Parisi, Editor of Poetry Magazine

Fourteen half-hour programs on seven cassettes with a 300-page *Listener's Guide*, including a biographical-critical essay on each poet, complete texts of all poems read in the series, and bibliographies.

Complete set in library slipcase: $85.00.
(Cassettes only: $65.00 *Listener's Guide* only: $9.95. Slipcase only: $10.00.)
(Postage and handling $3.00)

Modern Poetry Association
60 W. Walton St.
Chicago, IL 60610

POETS IN PERSON is made possible by a grant from the National Endowment for the Humanities with additional funding from Prince Charitable Trusts.

WHAT IS TOLD
A Novel
Askold Melnyczuk

ff Faber and Faber
50 Cross Street, Winchester MA 01890

SUBMISSION POLICIES

Ploughshares · Spring 1994

Ploughshares considers submissions postmarked between August 1 and March 31. All manuscripts sent from April to July are returned unread (we adhere very strictly to the postmark restrictions). Our address is: *Ploughshares,* Emerson College, 100 Beacon St., Boston, MA 02116-1596. *Ploughshares* is published three times a year: usually mixed issues of poetry and fiction in the Winter and Spring and a fiction issue in the Fall. Each is guest-edited by a different writer, who will often be interested in a specific theme. The thematic guidelines for the next reading period will be available in July, and to obtain them, you may either send a self-addressed, stamped envelope (s.a.s.e.) and ask for writer's guidelines, or call and listen to an announcement on our answering machine (*please do not phone before 7 p.m.:* 617-578-8753). More often than not, themes are designed to be as inclusive as possible. We usually read from August through November for the Spring issue, from November through February for the Fall issue, and from December through March for the Winter issue. You may submit for a specific issue, but please be timely, as we accumulate a backlog. Staff editors have the responsibility of determining for which issue/editor a work is most appropriate. If an issue closes, the work is considered for the next one(s). Overall, we look for submissions of serious literary value. For prose: one story, memoir, or personal essay. No criticism or book reviews. Novel excerpts are fine if they can be taken as short stories in themselves. Thirty-page maximum length. Typed double-spaced on one side of the page. For poetry: limit of 3-5 poems. Individually typed either single- or double-spaced on one side. (Sorry, but "Phone-a-Poem," 617-578-8754, is by invitation only.) Always submit prose and poetry separately. Only one submission each of nonfiction, fiction, and/or poetry at a time. Please do not send multiple submissions of the same genre for different issues/editors, and do not send another manuscript until you hear about the first. All manuscripts must first be screened at our office; never send directly to a guest editor. Please mail your manuscript in a page-sized manila envelope, your full name and address written on the outside, to the Fiction, Nonfiction, or Poetry Editor. All manuscripts and correspondence regarding submissions should be accompanied by an s.a.s.e. for reply or return of the manuscript, or we will not respond. Expect three to five months for a decision. Please do not query us on the status of a submission until five months have passed, and if you do, we prefer that you write to us, indicating the postmark date of submission, instead of calling. *We cannot accommodate revisions, changes of return address, or forgotten s.a.s.e.'s after the fact.* We do not reprint previously published work. Translations are welcome if permission has been granted. We cannot be responsible for delay, loss, or damage (usually postal-related). Never send originals or your only copy. Payment is upon publication: $10/printed page for prose, $20/page for poetry, $40 minimum per title, $200 maximum per author, with two copies of the issue and a one-year subscription.

**BENNINGTON
SUMMER
WRITING
WORKSHOPS**

July 3-July 16 &
July 17-July 30,
1994

■

ACADEMIC CREDIT
AVAILABLE

For more information, contact:
Liam Rector, Director
Bennington Summer Writing Workshops
Bennington College, Box S
Bennington, Vermont 05201
802-442-5401, ext. 160

FACULTY:

Douglas Bauer   Tom Jenks
Sven Birkerts   Elinor Lipman
Elizabeth Cox   Carole Maso
C. Michael Curtis   Kathleen Norris
Kate Daniels   Molly Peacock
Stephen Dobyns   Katha Pollitt
Lynn Freed   Bob Shacochis
Robert Grudin   Catherine Texier
Barry Hannah

READERS:

Charles Baxter   Donald Hall
Frank Bidart   Jane Kenyon
Lucie Brock-Broido   Liam Rector
David Broza   Mary Ruefle
Matthew Graham

**VISITING EDITORS
& LITERARY FOLK:**

D.W. Fenza   Askold Melnyczuk
Dan Halpern   Robin Moody
Stratis Haviaris   Peter Oresick
DeWitt Henry   Louisa Solano
Karl Kirchwey   Tamara Stock
Fiona McCrae   Scott Walker
Robert McDowell

Be an Expatriate Writer for Two Weeks.

Join a group of selected writers this summer for intensive fiction workshops in an exotic Dutch castle. With only twenty-five or so other seminar members, guided by five distinguished instructors, these two weeks are meant to be intimate and productive. In the mornings, short-story writers attend workshops, and novelists are individually advised on strategies for structure and revision, with the aim of completing publishable manuscripts. The afternoons are dedicated to private writing sessions and tutorials, ensuring that you will leave with new or honed work, as well as with redefined writing objectives. The evenings are set aside for readings and round-tables. Both the short-story and novel tracks concentrate on the craft and technique of fiction, and consider the pragmatics of the literary market. The dynamics of the seminar are carefully planned to include both published writers and those who are in the early stages of promising careers. The seminar is accredited for four academic credits and priced affordably. Inquire early to reserve your spot in this Renaissance castle. CO-DIRECTORS: Robie Macauley and Alexandra Marshall. FACULTY: James Carroll, Pamela Painter, and Thomas E. Kennedy, with a guest writer and visiting editor to be announced.

Fifth Annual

Ploughshares International Fiction Writing Seminar

*Castle Well
The Netherlands*

August 15–26, 1994

*Emerson College
European Center*

SHORT
STORY
CONTEST

The **Boston Review** is pleased to announce its second annual Short Story Contest. The winning entry will be published in the October 1994 issue of the **Boston Review** and will receive a cash prize of $300. The stories are not restricted by subject matter, should not exceed 4,000 words, and should be previously unpublished. There is a $10 processing fee, payable to the **Boston Review** in the form of a check or money order. All entrants receive a one-year subscription to the **Boston Review** beginning with the October issue. Submissions must be postmarked by August 1, 1994. Stories will not be returned. The winner will be notified by mail. Send your entry to: Short Story Contest, **Boston Review**, 33 Harrison Avenue, Boston, MA 02111.

the modern writer as witness

W I T N E S S

Special Issue

Sports in America

Volume VI Number 2 $7   1992

Contributors

Madison Smartt Bell

Siv Cedering

Jack Driscoll

Stuart Dybek

Tess Gallagher

George Garrett

Richard Hill

Maxine Kumin

Peter LaSalle

Paul Milenski

Heather Ross Miller

Jay Neugeboren

David Shields

Floyd Skloot

Mary Ann Waters

"Witness *is one of several excellent new literary and intellectual journals of the past few years that confirms our sense of the variety and scope of the imaginative life in the United States. Its focus upon thematic subjects is particularly valuable."*

Joyce Carol Oates

Call for Manuscripts:

Witness invites the submission of memoirs, essays, fiction, poetry and artwork for a special 1994 issue on **American Cities.** *Deadline: July 1, 1994.*

- Writings from *Witness* have been selected for inclusion in *Best American Essays, Best American Poetry, Prize Stories: The O. Henry Awards,* and *The Pushcart Prizes.*

- *Witness* will publish a special issue on **American Humor** in 1993.

W I T N E S S

Oakland Community College
Orchard Ridge Campus
27055 Orchard Lake Road
Farmington Hills, MI 48334

Individuals
1 yr/2 issues $12
2 yrs/4 issues $22

Institutions
1 yr/2 issues $18
2 yrs/4 issues $34